# VINES

English
**VINES**
(Horror/Fiction)
Yadu Vijayakrishnan

Published by
Quantic Creatives Private Limited.
Corporate Office: Quantic Nexus
TC 22/2459, SRL-A 68, Sankar Road, Sasthamangalam,
Thiruvananthapuram, Kerala 695010
Tel: 8289816366 | 8590011447
www.quanticcreatives.in

First published in September 2024


Layout: Qlife Infotech

Print: Akshara Offset, Trivandrum

ISBN: 978-81-969769-2-7

Price: ₹ 399

# VINES

**Yadu Vijayakrishnan**

'Open up! Open up! Help us!'

The screams of over a hundred staff members didn't leave the walls of the factory. The automated slaughterhouse, which produced meat from more than a thousand cows and buffalo a day, was closed shut. The employees found themselves trapped inside. The modern slaughterhouse was in the middle of nowhere. Away from civilization, there was no one to hear the cries for help.

'Tom....Tom...try calling the fire and rescue department,' Jacob, the supervisor, yelled at his assistant, who was already running to the office.

Tom didn't have time to reply to his supervisor. He was already on his way to call the rescue service since his phone was as good as dead; he needed the office phone.

'HELP!' Tom cried into the phone, 'Come to the Elite Meat Factory. We are trapped.'

'May I know the location, please?' the respondent was calm as a feather.

Despite being trembled and shaken, Tom gave the precise location of the slaughterhouse. He then ran back to Jacob.

'Sir, any idea what happened?' Tom was sweating like a waterfall.

Jacob gulped, 'I have no idea whatsoever.'

Jacob and Tom were standing at the upper level of the slaughterhouse, and they had a clear view of the other employees banging on the automated doors to open.

'When will help arrive?' Jacob asked.

'They said they need at least two hours to get here.' Tom wiped sweat from his eyebrows.

'I think we can wait till then.' Jacob relaxed and turned to his employees on the ground level, 'Everyone, attention please.'

The frantic staff members turned around. Those at the doors stopped trying to open them.

'There is no need to worry.' Jacob said as though he was a messiah, 'Help is on the way. Therefore, you all just need to relax.'

'How can we relax?' a man bellowed, 'We have the faintest idea of what happened! This is no electronic malfunction. Even the manual door at the fire exit is jammed. What if this is a terrorist attack?'

'If this was a terrorist attack, we all would've been dead by now,' Jacob said as loudly as he could. 'As you all know, this is a fairly new facility, and perhaps there might have been trouble in the construction and equipment. We need to maintain calm.'

Maintaining calm for them meant stopping running around in panic and refraining from banging heavily on the doors. But this didn't stop them from shouting and screaming at each other.

Usually, it was the cattle that made the loud noise inside the facility when they were carried to the chamber where they were killed. Then the noise would dissolve into the sounds of machines. The buzzing, scratching, hissing, and beeping of all the automated equipment inside the super modern house of slaughter used to reverberate inside. The cattle carcass automatic processing line, step-type conveyor, hydraulic peeling machine, and other devices that cut and chop living creatures came to a complete stop at this particular point in time.

It was such an ordinary day until everything went berserk. No single person in the facility was aware of what happened next. The lights went off and the machines stopped working. The automatic shutters closed down, and the manual ones were jammed as though some military force had purposefully quarantined the slaughterhouse staff.

'Let's see the technical guy,' Jacob said to Tom and walked towards a room full of computers and other sophisticated machines.

The technical guy, Ramesh, was repeatedly typing and clicking on the laptop in front of him. He was looking for an answer, but evidently, he didn't get any.

'The systems all seemed to work fine, but something tampered with the connection. Some other weird force overrode the system controls that led to the entire malfunctioning of the facility.' Ramesh panted, 'As all the machines here, the conveyor belts, the air conditioning, water pumping, everything, are centrally connected to this system, I can't manoeuvre anything. Even the power is lost completely, as you can see. We are all going to suffocate if we don't get out within a couple of hours. We are surviving by the sunlight coming from the glass windows below the roof. The ventilation isn't working. Right now, as we speak, we are breathing each other's breaths. But what I don't understand is how even the fire exits and manual doors are jammed. The security guards outside aren't responding as well.'

'Don't worry, help is on the way.' Jacob said, 'We'll be rescued within two hours.'

Jacob trudged to an isolated part of the facility. He dialled a contact that was on his phone.

'Hello,' the voice from the other end said. 'Didn't I tell you not to call me unless it's an emergency?'

'This is an emergency!' Jacob snapped quietly.

'What is it?' the rough voice asked.

'What kind of a hell hole did you put me into?' Jacob clenched his teeth.

'What do you mean?'

'This slaughterhouse you appointed me to look after,'

Jacob's words were as loud as they could be but as quiet as no one could hear, 'is literally a fragile structure. Who is the contractor?'

'See, Jacob, it's not a nuclear reactor or a power station, is it? It's just a place where cattle are killed. Why are you so worried about its construction all of a sudden?' the person on the phone said irritably, 'And please don't call me for such silly matters. I'm a politician and I don't want to be linked to this slaughterhouse in any way. We are all making something out of it, aren't we?'

'You earn politically and financially sitting in your cozy AC room while putting me in this bloodbath of animals. Don't forget what my family and I've done for you.' Jacob had a tight grip on the phone.

'Don't talk too much. You were broke. I was the one who put you in this position and you're now earning a decent salary. Be grateful for that.' the voice said, 'Just tell me what you want right now.'

'You guys have taken profit out of everything. This facility is poorly constructed and the automated technical system is faulty. We are suffocating in here.'

'That's it?' the voice laughed, 'This is what the emergency was? Report it to the management. They'll allot the funds needed to fix it. That's all it needs.'

'Excuse me if my voice sounded calm. The situation is more serious than you think. There are more than a hundred people working here and you've put all of our lives at stake in such poor working conditions. Sending an official report to the management and waiting for them to allot the funds and take subsequent measures will take time. I don't want that. I know with just one phone call you can get it all done.

Do it!'

'Are you threatening me?'

'Consider it so.'

'With what?'

'How about the information to the public that you are the owner of this slaughterhouse?' Jacob cautioned.

'Let's see.' The phone hung up after that.

Jacob was sweating. He didn't know whether it was caused by the extremely hot conditions inside or the conversation he had.

'Sir, sir.' Jacob saw Tom rushing towards him.

'What is it?' He didn't want to hear the answer.

'There is a problem!'

Tom took Jacob to the lower level where Ramesh and some other staff members were standing with arms like noodles.

'What happened?' Jacob asked, looking at everyone, 'What is that sound?'

Ramesh came forward, 'That's the problem. We have to keep it between us. The truth.'

What they were referring to was a whooshing sound.

'Isn't it the sound of some running machine or conveyor belt or something? Maybe it's some backup generator.' Jacob wasn't confident of what he said.

'Sir, the power supply of the facility is down completely,' Tom replied, 'Not even the generators are working. This isn't the sound of a machine.'

'Enough with the dramatics,' Jacob glowered, 'Tell me what the problem is.'

'It's a leak,' Tom came forward.

'It's carbon dioxide,' Ramesh added.

'How is this possible?' Jacob said, his loss of energy evident from his voice.

'I'm not sure,' Tom stammered, 'But it seems the valves or pipes carrying CO2 meant to stun animals unconscious in their chambers are broken. That's the only way.'

'Who did that? This all seems to be the activities of someone. How can things fall apart one after the other?' Jacob found it hard to speak.

'Sir, we will all be dead even before the rescue arrives!' Tom moaned. 'But panic won't solve our problems.'

Jacob lumbered forward and saw the staff of the slaughterhouse talking to each other cluelessly.

'We have to maintain calm, alright,' Jacob said. 'But our death is certain.'

'Please do not inform the others,' Ramesh begged.

'Everything is over. There is no point in anything. We've been killing hundreds of living beings here for the past few months. It's our turn now.'

Tom and Ramesh gawked at Jacob.

Jacob trudged to his employees and said at the top of his voice, 'It's CO2! It's leaking. We're all going to be dead within minutes!'

As if a machine started working, the noise inside the facility rose in decibels in a matter of seconds. They were running in all directions they could find. The noise of cries and screams of human beings echoed inside the slaughterhouse.

Jacob didn't stop walking. He climbed the upper layer and watched everything. However, he noticed his sight getting blurred as though he was seeing ghosts. He felt dizzy. His legs wobbled and he lay down. Yet he could see the employees vomiting, crying, and floundering around. Some of them collapsed. Some of them continued banging on the doors, screaming.

Jacob's consciousness slowly drifted to nothingness.

As the analogue clock of the slaughterhouse ticked forward, the noise inside fainted and came to a complete silence.

# 02

You have to apply force to make the action worthwhile, but be as gentle as possible so as not to destroy the entire thing. What a dilemma! What should be destroyed and what should be kept? Try identifying that if you're a palaeontologist or an archaeologist. The job is easier for an archaeologist, though. Fortunately for Avinash Mahadevan, he is an archaeologist. Avinash is currently at the ancient Indian city of Kirtipuri, or rather, the ruins of it. Kirtipuri spans half a kilometre in radius inside a forest reserve in the state of Madhya Pradesh. There are tanks, drainages, towers, temples, citadels, and a palace. Yet, it is all green. Covered by thick vines and strangler figs, the brown buildings stand as a testimony to nature's victory over man-made objects.

The area was left unnoticed after it was abandoned by the inhabitants almost 1,000 years ago. Therefore, there weren't any conquerors or colonialists to reclaim the land and demolish the buildings to build new ones. For that reason, a small portion of the city still stands, but at the mercy of nature.

'We have to carefully remove the vines and strangler figs,' Prof. Ahmed, the chief archaeologist, said. 'And we have to make sure we place supporting bricks or beams so that the entire structure won't collapse.'

The thick roots and strangler figs grew in between the buildings and deformed them all. These tentacles of nature are now the backbone of these ancient monuments. Prof. Ahmed, also called the Heritage Man, knows perfectly how to excavate such historical sites. This is not an excavation in the sense that the site is being reclaimed from the ground. Maybe that is why they are planning to assemble local daily wage labourers who would usually clear up forests.

Avinash is fairly new to excavations. He had just finished his archaeology course. He served as an intern in many excavations during his studies. Anyhow, this was an entirely new experience for him. He had been part of several missions to reclaim structures from deep below the earth, but this was the first time he was seeing something swallowed by the forest.

'This is not the first time such reclamation of historic sites has been done,' Ahmed said to Avinash. 'The medieval city of Vijayanagara was also in a similar condition until the ruins were discovered by Colin Mackenzie in the early 19th century.'

Vijayanagara was a textbook subject for Indian historians and archaeologists. It is one of UNESCO's World Heritage Sites as well. Obviously, Ahmed didn't need to explain anything further to Avinash.

However, the city of Kirtipuri is extraordinary. It has been undiscovered for over a thousand years. The date was found through historic texts, though. No carbon dating of artefacts has been done to identify the exact period of the city. The case is understood anyway. Just like the cities of the Indus Valley Civilization and Vijayanagara, as soon as the inhabitants abandoned the city, nature took over it.

'And I have firsthand experience reclaiming such a site before,' Ahmed said proudly.

'Really? Where?' Avinash curiously asked.

'That was here in Madhya Pradesh too. Sarweshwar group of monuments.'

'Yeah, I've heard about it,' Avinash said, clearly impressed. 'It was indeed a monumental task, wasn't it?'

'Of course, but it didn't end well,' Ahmed replied, bowing his head down.

'What happened, sir?'

'Well, the mining mafia around the area continued blasting their explosives,' Ahmed said, irritated. 'All that we managed to recover started to crumble piece by piece.'

'Once again, humans have become their own villains,' Avinash said flatly.

'True!' Ahmed said, brushing off some dirt on a stone fragment on the ground. 'Humans aren't just villains of their own story. They are torturing the planet as well. Earth is on the verge of destruction thanks to human activities.'

'There is no point in all those protests of environmental

activists,' Avinash said slowly, with some doubt. 'Most of them are doing it for their own publicity. There has been no positive change in the environment lately. What do we do?'

'We don't need to do anything!'

'What do you mean? Just staying passive will help the situation?' Avinash cleaned his spectacles with the lower end of his shirt.

'I meant we humans don't need to do anything. Nature will do the necessary for correcting everything to order. Nature has its own format and restart button. Once it is activated, all our advanced technology will be shredded into pieces.'

'Sir, is it another theory you're proposing?' the young man said jokingly.

'No, boy, it's even mentioned in the spiritual texts of Hinduism, isn't it?' Ahmed said while slowly walking to a ruin of a temple. 'Hindu scriptures always mentioned the self-refreshment of the universe. After every 4 yugas, the world will start a new phase, clearing up everything that was left before. On top of that, Lord Vishnu himself said he will visit Earth whenever evil stands prevalent.'

'Wait a second!' Avinash frowned. 'Lord Vishnu said he will take an incarnation on Earth whenever humans are in danger at the hands of evil Asuras.'

'Really? Did he say that?' Ahmed replied with a smile. 'In the Bhagavad Gita, speaking as the human form of Krishna, Lord Vishnu said he'll come whenever Dharma is in danger. Dharma means virtue, right behaviour, and social order. It also means when Adharma, or evil, is dominant. If we humans are this Adharma, then how will Vishnu save us? He'll clearly wipe us out to save the planet.'

Ahmed began laughing after that, and his laughter gradually faded as he neared a ruin of a shrine.

'Hmm...the idol is missing in this shrine,' Ahmed scratched his chin. 'Which god do you think this belongs to?'

'By the look of it...' Avinash looked inside the ruined empty sanctum sanctorum. 'Let's find any other sculpture around here. Maybe that will lead us.'

'Correct!'

Ahmed tasked his junior archaeologists and labourers to carefully excavate the area around the ruined shrine. A small sculpture of a bull appeared from the first layer itself.

Being the chief archaeologist, Ahmed took the sculpture and placed it in front of a small platform in front of the shrine. With some mild cracks here and there, the base of the sculpture suited the depression of the platform.

'And this means?' Ahmed asked.

'It's a Shrine of Shiva,' answered Avinash. 'Each god in Hinduism has a mode of transport. For Vishnu, it's Garuda. For Durga, it's a tiger. For Ganesh, it's a rat, and for Shiva, it's the bull Nandi.'

'So this is how archaeologists work to identify temples and monuments?' the contractor who brought the labourers chipped in.

'Exactly!' Ahmed replied with pride. 'We need to study the

scriptures and the culture of our civilization to preserve it.'

'That means you know all about Lord Shiva?' the contractor asked.

'Sure...and all other gods of Hinduism too,' Ahmed said. 'Lord Shiva is my favourite as he looks after the divine duty of destruction.'

'Divine destruction? Sir? How can destruction be divine?' Thomas, one of the archaeologists, asked.

'Destruction is inevitable.' Ahmed took out his smartphone. 'Just as you clear out all those unwanted cache files, WhatsApp pics, and applications to make room for important apps or just as when all these files in your phone memory are making it slow and corrupt, you'll end up completely formatting the phone to its original factory settings. Isn't all that destruction done on a positive note? So on a cosmic level, such destruction is divine.'

At the same time, Avinash felt his phone vibrating. He usually doesn't check out his phone during work, but he decided to go against his nature and took it out. It was just a Facebook message. He didn't care to open it and subsequently put it back in his pocket.

The young man felt the vibration once again and ignored it. He felt it a third time and opened it.

As he didn't have a separate app for Facebook messages, he opened the Facebook Lite app, which takes less data and storage. The message was from a girl, Alma Fatima. It appeared that she was his Facebook friend. Yet, he had no idea when he accepted her friend request. Anyways, he didn't go on to read what the message was. He could, however, see the preview of the last message she sent.

It was: 'Aren't you not?'

Avinash was back in his room. It was a bungalow run by the government as a guest house for government employees. His chief was also staying in the bungalow but in another room. Avinash had his dinner, a few rotis, and sabji. As he is from the southern state of Kerala, rotis weren't exactly his favourite meal.

The room was clean and perfectly set by the staff of the guest house. The young archaeologist just needed to lie down on the comfy bed to fall asleep immediately, but he opted to check out his Facebook before that.

That is when he remembered the strange message from Alma Fatima. Who is that?

He didn't care about any other updates. He went right ahead to read the messages.

It appeared as though this Alma Fatima had been messaging him for months.

Sure enough, she had been sending him Hi, Hai, Hello, Hai, Hi, and so on.

Avinash Mahadevan would normally ignore such messages, especially from one without a profile picture of a human being.

It is common to find fake profiles on Facebook, especially in the name of girls. As the guys who make these accounts don't have a valid image of a girl, they either put a photo of a celebrity actress or something else like a flower or a butterfly as profile pictures. In the case of Alma Fatima, it was a picture of a cartoon cat.

But what struck Avinash's attention is that Alma Fatima had also sent some personal questions like: ‘Aren't you the Avinash Mahadevan who studied in SN Public School?’ and ‘Aren't you the Avinash Mahadevan who won the inter-school quiz competition?’

‘Alright,’ Avinash thought, ‘Even if this is a fake account, it belongs to someone who knows me really well.’

‘Hai!’ Avinash wrote, and his fingers lingered on the keypad of his smartphone, but he didn't proceed with writing any further. It was already past 11 pm, and Avinash wasn't in a mood to chat. He placed his phone beside the pillow and lied down.

The phone vibrated again. And again.

Avinash rolled back and checked it. Just as he anticipated, it was Alma's reply.

This time, it wasn't just texts. They were audio clips.

‘Hey, do you remember me? I was in 9th when you were studying in 12th,’ the sweet feminine voice asked.

Avinash was convinced that this wasn't a fake account.

‘I don't remember your name, honestly,’ Avinash recorded and sent his voice after checking out Alma Fatima's profile in detail. There wasn't a single photo of her there.

Any other guy would've asked for Alma's photo, but Avinash wasn't that guy.

'Oh! It's alright. I wasn't popular or anything there. You were the famous one, that's why I know you.'

Avinash felt somebody tickling him all around. He never felt he was popular in school. On the contrary, he actually thought he was a kind of ignored geek there. Most of his friends had a girlfriend. He didn't have any. Although he had a crush on a girl, he didn't have the guts to ask her out. Neither did any girl approach him. So he felt he was only a nerd who no one was interested in.

However, when Avinash entered college, he started getting messages from girls on Facebook who were with him in school. His looks had a radical change with the addition of a beard. The frame of his spectacles became fashionable through the years too. The same guy who couldn't manage to speak to a girl for ten minutes straight went on to chat for hours. He built a sort of confidence after that.

Still, he never believed he was popular in school.

They continued to chat for a while, but Avinash had trouble using both text and audio recording.

'Uh..Alma, good night then. I have trouble sending messages in this Facebook Lite app. I don't want to install the separate Messenger app either,' Avinash sent his voice.

'It's alright. We can use WhatsApp then. I hope you have that,' she replied.

Really? Avinash had a principle: never to ask for the WhatsApp number of a woman unless it's related to profession or something serious. He never liked the idea of chatting with someone (especially women) for the sake of chatting. Even in college, while all others had each other's numbers, Avinash only kept those he needed and those who needed him. While his roommates were busy chatting with girls at midnight, he spent nights either reading or sleeping.

Anyhow, when a girl asked for his number, he wouldn't hesitate to give his contact.

Just a minute later, Avinash found himself chatting with Alma on WhatsApp.

'So, are you studying or what?' Avinash asked.

'I'm doing a master's in psychology.'

'Wow! Great!' Avinash said, but Alma couldn't see his eyes getting wider. 'You should pursue a PhD after this.'

Alma didn't reply to that. Instead, she talked about the events they had in their school.

Finally, when Avinash yawned, he realized he needed to wake up the next morning to continue his duty at the excavation site.

'Let's sleep then, Alma. Good night,' he texted.

'It's actually good morning,' the reply voice clip announced. 'It's already 5 am.'

That's when Avinash realized how time had gone by without himself being aware of it. He couldn't even recall the details of the conversation they had for the past few hours.

The professor is going to kill me if I don't wake up on time.

# 03

Nehru Colony, formerly known as Manal Slums, usually wouldn't have any visitors. The exception is at the time of elections. when candidates, along with their party workers from different political parties, visit each house in the slum and promise a bright future if they get elected. The inhabitants of the colony would see these visitors again after five years, right before the next elections.

This was not such a day. There weren't any elections close by. However, a group of seven men, dressed neatly in formal political attire, sauntered through the colony. All of them were carrying bags of groceries except one person. A tall, bearded man with spectacles walked among his fellows but at the dead centre.

'Comrade Ragesh, we have about twenty more houses left,' a guy from the group called out. 'We don't have enough supplies to distribute to all of them.'

'It's alright,' Ragesh Nakutty said, walking straight ahead without turning around to his comrade. 'We can visit here on another day and donate the rest.'

The group turned left at a cross ahead and entered a shanty where they were greeted by an old couple. The old woman extended a plastic armchair to Ragesh. One of the comrades gave a bag of groceries to the woman. The old man was lying on a bed in the same room.

'He is paralyzed,' the old woman said.

'Oh, I see,' Ragesh looked at the old man, who leaned his head at a right angle to see him.

'Son, when did you return from Delhi?' the old woman asked with respect and affection.

'No... no...' Comrade Ragesh replied with a certain irritation. 'I'm not a member of parliament anymore.'

'Comrade Ragesh lost the last election,' a fellow comrade chipped in.

Ragesh turned around to stare at him, and the fellow froze still as though Ragesh's laser eyes had damaged his senses.

'The opposition party tampered with the electronic voting machine. That's why I lost,' Ragesh defended.

'Oh, son, we don't have a TV or newspaper here. We didn't know,' the old woman said.

'Comrade is so popular that even people with TVs and newspapers consider him as their representative in parliament,' the same fellow comrade added.

'I know how good you are, son. You've gifted us these groceries. This will feed us for a month,' the old woman said with tears. 'You are so great that you have spent your own money to give this to such ignored people like us.'

'It is the nature of our Comrade Ragesh Nakutty. He is benevolent and generous,' a guy from the comrade group said loudly.

'I understand, son. You will win the next election for sure. Good people like you shouldn't be defeated. God will not allow that,' the old woman cheered.

'Yes, without the support from you all, I can never win,' Comrade Ragesh said with a smile and got up. 'I wish I could stay here longer, but I have other houses to visit. I kindly take your leave.'

The comrade group was on the alley. They distributed the rest of the grocery kits and returned to their cars parked outside Nehru Colony. Comrade Ragesh sat in his favourite seat of the brand-new Innova Crysta.

'How many more supply kits do we have at the party office?' Ragesh asked.

'Not enough,' comrade Sumesh replied with certainty while driving the car.

'Okay, then stop at PDI warehouse on the way back,' Ragesh said to the driver. 'Our union labourers are there right now. I will call others to go there as well.'

The three cars rushed through the busy streets of the city to the outskirts where it was comparatively calmer. The Innova Crysta, with a red board in front declaring 'Ex-MP,' parked around 400 meters away from the PDI warehouse. Yet, the two other cars, one of which picked Ragesh from Innova, went ahead and parked at the back of the warehouse.

A group of sweaty labourers came out from the warehouse and bowed, seeing Comrade Ragesh in front of them.

'It's an honor to see you, comrade. We didn't know you would come here personally,' a labourer said. 'We have already packed them according to the requirements.'

'Who is taking care of the inventory and accounts?' Ragesh enquired.

'That would be our overseer, Mr. Sivakumar. Don't worry, he is our guy,' the labourer said.

'Call him,' Ragesh said flatly.

A man came rushing outside within a few minutes. He wasn't sweaty at all.

'Comrade Ragesh, is everything fine?' Sivakumar extended his arm, implying a handshake.

Ragesh didn't hold the supervisor's hand. 'Everything's not fine. That's why I came here personally to see you.'

'What happened, sir?'

'What happened? Don't you know?' Ragesh bellowed. 'Are you not the kind of person who is aware of political memes circulating on social media? Here, see this.'

Ragesh spent another half a minute clicking and swiping repeatedly on his phone, then he gave the phone to the overseer. It was a news report from a less popular news portal.

The Leftist party is hoarding government supplies in their party offices and distributing them as their own. The central government started supplying groceries and other essential items to be distributed to people belonging to economically backward regions. Unfortunately, the ruling party of the state has misused their power to transfer the supplies and distribute the same supplies without using government machinery. Furthermore, they are 'donating' the kits as if they were sponsored by their leaders. There are some reports of the kits being distributed to undeserving people close to the party workers.

'You read that?' Ragesh said, unable to control his rage. 'Fortunately, the report was published by a not-so-popular news portal considered unreliable. But I want to know how this news got out?'

'I'm sorry, sir,' Sivakumar trembled. 'I personally manage the inventory list and accounts so that no one will know. This must have leaked by someone else.'

'So you're saying it's not your responsibility to stop that leak?'

'No, sir. I was saying that it's beyond the scope of my control,' the supervisor was still trembling.

'Tell me, how did you get this job?'

'I was a clerk in Cashew Corporation. Got promoted to this position,' Sivakumar said without much pride.

'I know you got promoted. You weren't born an overseer. Tell me HOW you got promoted?' Ragesh asked, expecting an immediate answer.

'With the help of the Party, sir. I overtook another person who was in line for the promotion,' Sivakumar replied.

'So you are aware of that fact?' Ragesh said sarcastically. 'Then isn't it your responsibility to prevent any information that could harm the Party that helped you?'

'Definitely, sir. I will be extra vigilant,' Sivakumar replied immediately and confidently.

'Alright then. You can go. Be careful from now on. I don't want to come here more often.'

Ragesh said and turned around to his comrades. 'Go get the supply kits. I'm exhausted.'

'Comrade, you can leave. We will take care of this,' a comrade from the group said positively.

Ragesh was dropped at the point where the Innova Crysta was parked. Like before, Sumesh got into the driving seat. The MUV was cooled with a high volume of air conditioning.

'Comrade, I thought you were planning to change constituencies in the next parliament election?' Sumesh asked with a slight fear of bringing down the wrath of the ex-MP.

'Who told you I want to contest in the next parliament election?' Ragesh replied with his eyes on the road. 'I don't want to be an MP again. I got used to it, bored actually, being in that position for ten years.'

'So, what is your next plan, comrade?' Sumesh asked. 'If you don't mind sharing it with me. I'm still your PA, right?'

'I'm not actually interested in being a member of anything, whether it be the parliament or the assembly,' Ragesh declared. 'Either be the leader of the Party or the State. Until I'm able to achieve that, I'll be the puppeteer.'

'Sir, but aren't there many senior leaders in line for the Chief Minister post? The current CM won't definitely come back after his term. But even then, there are comrade Sasi, Newton, Gopalan, Haji, and Sulekha who are competing for the chair,' Sumesh took his eyes from the road and looked at his comrade. 'Isn't the parliament membership the best for you at this point in time?'

'See Sumesh, our Party has four members in the parliament, which has a total of 545 seats. The Party is neither in power nor significant in any other state of the country. So, being a Member of Parliament means that you are worth as a worm despite being at the receiving end of government-level privileges. Whereas, if you're the Chief Minister of this state, that means you have unlimited power. It is the last of the communist strongholds in the entire world. The person ruling this state has connections with international communist nations and organizations. Additionally, his name will be written in history books.'

'Comrade, but how will you convince all those senior leaders to make way for you to the chair? Will they agree?' Sumesh gasped.

'Dear Sumesh, there is nothing money can't buy.' Ragesh, for the first time, turned his attention from the road and smiled at his PA.

'But that means you have to give them hundred thousands

of Rupees.' Sumesh exclaimed, 'Where will you raise that kind of money?'

'It will cost me millions.' Comrade Ragesh stated, 'And I can raise that.'

'Where do you want to go next, comrade?' asked Sumesh.

'There is one more job to do today,' said Ragesh. 'Take me to Arisumkadavu Ecological Park. There are comrades waiting for me.'

It was a one and half hour long drive to Arisumkadavu Ecological Park.

'How many were you able to assemble?' Ragesh asked someone on phone, 'No, fifty isn't enough. Mobilize at least two hundred comrades.'

Sumesh wondered if Ragesh is going to lead some sort of protest against the organization running the park due to some anti-labour policies. Although he was curious, he wasn't brave enough to ask Ragesh about it.

They reached the Arisumkadavu Ecological Park where Ragesh was welcomed by a hundred comrades. Some of them were carrying cans of kerosene.

'Where are the others?' Ragesh asked the Branch Secretary of the party.

'Sorry, comrade. Only this much showed up,' replied the Branch Secretary.

'Are there any security officers for the park?' asked Ragesh.

'Just three watchmen and maybe about ten employees. They are all unarmed. They won't pose any challenge.'

'Alright. You know, there was no need for me to come here, but I just wanted to see how much we got. MK Madhavan split up the party and some of our workers have left with him leaving our party and there are still people loyal to him. He won the regional election defeating our candidate and I want to make sure we still have our comrades with us. Anyways, don't tell anyone that I brought this idea. You guys do it. The party leadership will be proud of you guys. I don't want any credits,' said Ragesh to the Branch Secretary walking him to another side of road.

Ragesh got in the car and left.

The Branch Secretary and other comrades stormed into the ecological park where the watchmen found themselves helpless in stopping them. First they went into the snake chambers and shattered the glasses of each exhibits. They poured the kerosene with a steady hand, the pungent liquid spilled over the slithering bodies. The comrades flicked a lighter and let it fall. The fire caught instantly, racing along the kerosene-soaked scales and consumed the snakes in an instant. The vipers thrashed and hissed their last breaths lost beneath the roar of the fire.

The employees of the park tried to stop the madness but they were physically assaulted by the activists.

The mob then went to the nearby exhibits where exotic and rare birds were caged. Molotov cocktail was thrown and the exhibits start to burn with the vulnerability of the lush foliage. With it, the birds also burned to death.

The mob surged forward and advanced on to the next target - the aviary.

Inside the aviary, the exotic birds, rare and beautiful, flitted anxiously in their cages, sensing the encroaching danger. The air there was thick with the scent of damp earth and fragrant, lush foliage.

A comrade stepped forward, a Molotov cocktail gripped tightly in his hand. With a quick, practiced motion, he lit the rag stuffed into the bottle's neck and the bottle was hurled toward the cages. It shattered on impact, the fire exploding outward in a violent burst. The flames leaped eagerly to the foliage, feeding hungrily on the dry leaves and wooden perches.

The birds shrieked and their wings beating frantically against the confines of their cages. The fire spread engulfing everything in its path. The screeches grew more frantic, more desperate, but there was no escape. The metal bars sealed their fate, trapping them in a burning hell.

The mob watched, their faces expressionless as the blaze consumed the aviary. The exhibit was reduced to smouldering ash, the rare and exotic birds nothing more than charred remnants of what once was.

Satisfied, the mob turned away, their work done. They left the inferno behind, the destruction complete, moving as one to the next target, leaving nothing but devastation in their wake.

Two hours of relentless vandalism left a trail of devastation. Rare reptiles - twelve cobras, two king cobras, and monitor lizards were perished in the inferno, their scales charred beyond recognition. Migratory birds, including painted and grey storks, peacocks, vultures, eagles, and several mynah species, were caught in the blaze, their vibrant feathers reduced to ash. Even the small, innocent rabbits could not escape the flames.

The horror did not end there. Some snakes, managing to slither free from the fire's grasp, were met with a brutal fate. Leftist Party workers hunted them down and stoned them to death, ensuring no life escaped their wrath.

The photos of the dead animals accompanied with the news Arisumkadavu Ecological Park Attacked! The Park is run by the NGO in which former Leftist Party leader Madhavan serves as the President.

# 04

A rusty-looking semi-truck escorted by two dusty but brand-new SUVs arrived at an ugly concrete building among other similar structures in a valley of dry plateaus. The semi-truck was carrying what seemed to be a load of hay. Six guys, clearly not in a good mood, got out of the SUVs and entered the concrete building. They spent about thirty minutes inside and returned with a couple dozen sacks. They loaded the sacks onto the semi-truck and hid them with the hay.

The semi-truck and the two SUVs left the valley and entered the state highway on top of a plateau. The region didn't have much greenery to hide the vehicles. The dry Central Indian landscape had a few isolated, parched trees randomly distributed on the terrain.

'You see there,' the rough guy sitting on the pillion seat pointed to a hill afar, 'that's where we're going to blow up.'

'For rocks?' the driver asked.

'What?' the rough guy was shocked. 'Oh... you're the new

guy Asif bhai sent, aren't you?'

'Yes,' the driver replied. 'My name is Tarbar.'

'So, didn't Asif bhai tell you what we are supposed to do?'

'He said we're going to blow up a hill for mining, and we have to be discreet about it as we are doing it illegally,' Tarbar said. 'But he didn't tell me what we are mining.'

'So, if that's all Asif bhai told you, then that's all you need to know,' the rough guy replied. 'And my name is Vishal Shukla. I'm handling this operation.'

'Oh... I know you, sir,' Tarbar said with high regard. 'Asif bhai told me about you.'

'Hmmm... therefore, you don't need to know anything else about this mission,' Shukla said while looking straight at the hills ahead.

'If you don't mind, sir, can you please tell me why we aren't carrying any explosives for the blasting? Shouldn't dynamite be used?' Tarbar was clearly confused.

'We've already loaded our truck behind us with explosives,' Shukla said. 'It's hidden by the hay.'

'What?' Tarbar became more confused. 'I thought those sacks were cement or something.'

'No... no... those aren't cement sacks. Those are explosives,' Shukla declared. 'Dynamite is an old technique. This is the modern way. ANFO! Ammonium Nitrate Fuel Oil. Each sack has 25 kilograms of it. It's hard to get it in the black market, but I managed it.'

As the fleet moved with the semi-truck between the two SUVs, two cops under the scrawny shade of a tree with their parked police car extended their arms, trying to stop the semi-truck. The truck stopped and parked at the point where the cops directed it. Meanwhile, the two SUVs continued moving forward but parked around 200 meters away from the cops.

'What are you carrying?' a cop with a thick moustache questioned the driver of the truck.

'Just hay, sir.'

'We need to check. Come out.'

The driver got off the truck and walked towards the back.

The other cop, a clean-shaven guy, saw the two SUVs parked ahead.

'Hey... I need to check this. I feel something suspicious about those cars,' the beardless cop bellowed to his colleague and started walking toward the parked SUVs.

'We didn't tell you to stop, did we?' he asked Vishal Shukla. 'The car in front of you, is that your company too?'

'No, we just wanted a break. That is why we stopped,' Vishal said without stammering.

Meanwhile, the semi-truck was being scrutinized by the other cop.

'What's inside the hay?' the cop asked.

'Sir, what do you mean?' the driver stammered. 'It's nothing but hay.'

'Take out the bunches at the edge,' the cop sneered.

Hearing the commotion, the beardless cop turned to look at the semi-truck. Vishal Shukla got out of the SUV and saw the truck's driver almost begging the cop who was questioning him.

'Hey, why did you get out of the car?' the shaved cop said irritably.

'Alright!' Shukla bowed down and reached for something under the pillion seat. He took out a three-foot iron rod and slammed it right on the head of the cop in front of him. Pressing his hand on his head, the officer cried for help.

The cop at the truck left the driver and started running towards the injured cop.

'Go! Go! Go!' Vishal screeched while getting inside his SUV. The semi-truck and the two SUVs left the place as if they were launched space shuttles.

'Officer injured! Mafia spotted! We need backup!' the cop repeated on his wireless.

The mafia fleet was dashing through the state highway alone until they were joined by three police cars with loud sirens. Perhaps the SUVs could outrun the police cars, but they were sure that the semi-truck didn't have the horsepower to do the same.

'We need to deceive them,' Vishal said to Tarbar. 'Their attention should be diverted to our cars and not the truck. We must let them chase us and leave the truck. I will call the others and do the necessary.'

The two SUVs decelerated and let their semi-truck overtake them and move ahead. The SUVs drove at a slower pace side by side, blocking the entire width of the highway. The police cars in hot pursuit found their trail to the semi-truck blocked by this battle formation of the SUVs. However, one of the three police cars drove off the pavement and overtook the SUVs by riding on the rough terrain. It found itself on the smooth pavement of the highway within no time.

'I will manage these two. You guys take care of the one following the truck,' Vishal said to someone on the phone.

Immediately, one of the SUVs broke the formation and accelerated ahead. The other one made way on the left side of the road. In this gap, a police car tried to cut across. Vishal was waiting for that moment. He aimed his pistol at the wheel of the overtaking police car and pulled the trigger without any hesitation. The SUV dashed forward, making space for the wrecked police car to skid across the road, rolling over and finally falling off the pavement. Whether anyone was injured or not is unknown. Nonetheless, the third police car stopped by the wreckage to save the lives of their fellow officers.

Vishal's SUV joined the race. He saw the police car trying to outrun the SUV towards the truck, but the giant SUV was repeatedly crashing into the side of the police car, slowing it down. Barely a few minutes passed, and the police car found itself between the two big SUVs and was repeatedly being hammered by both of them. The damage forced it to a complete halt, and the officers inside saw the truck disappearing in the distance. Two cops jumped out and began shooting at the SUVs, but they only managed to hit the road and the doors. The SUVs left the place, leaving no trails behind.

'The pursuit isn't over,' Vishal said to someone on the phone. 'Two other police cars are coming. I saw them. We won't reach there before they catch us. You must take a diversion and hide the explosives somewhere. We will go straight, acting as bait for the cops, leading them nowhere until we lose the hook. You should only come to Asif bhai's den at midnight.'

A few hundred meters ahead, the semi-truck took a left turn and entered a path that wasn't tarred. The truck disappeared into the sparse forest with dry trees and bushes. In the meantime, two other police cars were chasing the SUVs that were racing through the lone highway.

The SUVs never reached their potential speed; instead, they slowed down sometimes and rushed forward as if they were teasing the police cars and wasting their time. The hot pursuit went on for another twenty minutes until the drivers of the SUVs shifted gears and stepped on the gas pedal without pity.

Five minutes past midnight.

Asif bhai and Vishal Shukla were enjoying their fourth peg of Officer's Choice in the dark outside an old degraded mansion. They were put into a spotlight by an arriving vehicle, apparently, the semi-truck.

'Were you checked by any cops after that?' Shukla asked the driver.

'Yes, sir. Luckily, as you told me to hide the explosives and change the number plates, the cops couldn't find anything on the truck,' the driver said. 'They were checking each and every truck that passed by after our incident.'

'I knew that would happen,' Shukla said with pride. 'That's why I told you to hide it and come here later.' He then turned to Asif, 'We can take the ANFO tomorrow and postpone the drilling and blasting for next week. Isn't that okay, Asif bhai?'

'Perfectly fine,' Asif said, shaking his shoulders.

'Tomorrow, we aren't taking the truck or the SUVs. They are looking for every vehicle similar to ours. Instead, we should take the four jeeps here. Go to the hiding spot separately, load the explosives onto the jeeps, and come here. Wait for another week, and once the cops get busy with another rape case, we'll blow up the hill.'

'Brilliant!' Asif bhai shook his shoulders after gulping down another peg.

The sun was mercilessly torturing the people in the region the next day. But it wasn't any excuse for Vishal and his team. Four different-looking jeeps, tattered and rusted, arrived at an eerie-looking location in the sparse wild.

'Where is it?' Vishal asked the driver.

'I dug it up here. Beneath this dry tree. I even marked the tree. Look,' the driver trembled.

Yes, there was a marking etched on the tree. But on the ground, it was covered with thick vegetation.

'How did you dig here without breaking the vines on top?' Vishal asked furiously.

'I swear, there were no vines here at that time. Let's dig up, and I'll show you.' The driver called the other drivers of the jeeps.

They carefully cut the vines and shovelled off the dirt. But no matter how deep they removed the thick soil, nothing but dry roots were seen.

'Are you sure you hid them here?' Vishal scratched his head.

'Sir, I promise on my mother. I dug here. It took me more than half an hour. I carefully placed the sacks. Covered it all with the same dirt. Marked this tree and left,' the driver was confident this time, but he was frightened.

'Then where is it?' Vishal snapped. 'All I can see is nothing but good-for-nothing vines.'

As it was an isolated region, there weren't any inhabitants. It's a place where no visitors are attracted. The only visitors the place had after a long time were the rough-looking guys who came searching for some sacks. And they were the only people dead from the explosion that no one knows who detonated or how it happened.

'Woke up late?' Ahmed asked with a slight smile while sipping tea, an empty breakfast plate in front of him.

'Sorry, sir.' Avinash quickly grabbed a seat and sat opposite his chief.

The caretaker of the guest house served aloo roti to Avinash, and the young archaeologist immediately started munching on it.

Less than half an hour later, the Toyota Innova took Ahmed and Avinash to the site of Kirtipuri. They immediately started working once they reached there.

However, Avinash took out his phone to check for updates. He was disappointed to find nothing more than some spam messages. As time progressed, Avinash became more and more irritated. This was reflected in his behaviour towards the labourers. The usually calm guy walked around the site, losing his focus here and there.

The young archaeologist couldn't concentrate. He couldn't eat his lunch properly. As a result, he finished sooner than everyone else and had time to spare. He ambled to a banyan tree and sat down. He took out his phone and opened WhatsApp.

Nope! No text from Alma.

Avinash checked the status tab and began looking at the multimedia statuses his friends had uploaded. With the poor network connectivity in the area, it took a while for the pictures to load. That's when he came across Alma Fatima's status.

There were multiple photographs of a gorgeous girl in a hijab.

They all appeared to be screenshots of statuses uploaded by others.

One image read, 'Happy Birthday Almaa.' Another one had full graphical text on the photo of the hijab-wearing girl: 'Happy Birthday Almoooo.' About ten similar screenshots followed.

This was the first time Avinash got a chance to see the girl he had talked to for hours the previous night. The elegantly decorated hijab only exposed part of her face, but that was enough to invoke wonder in his mind. Her cheeks were like strawberries, and her eyes were dazzling. Her lips seemed softer than anything he had felt before. The young man was staring at the photos for a long time until he was brought back to the present by the sound of his chief's voice.

While he was walking back to the ruin of a shrine, Avinash sent a message to Alma.

'Didn't know it was your birthday today! Happy Birthday, Alma!'

Avinash returned to his job, analysing the vines, roots, and strangler figs that entwined the ruins.

He felt his phone vibrating several times after that. He was in the middle of instructing the labourers about the excavation and couldn't take out his phone. Avinash quickly finished that session and moved to a shaded area. As expected, there were voice replies from Alma.

'Thank you. You know one thing? You were chatting with me the whole first hour of my birthday. It was really special. I will never forget this 24th birthday of mine.'

Perhaps this was the first time Avinash thought he had become special to a girl. It had not been 24 hours since he started chatting with her, and he was already feeling butterflies in his stomach. He very much wanted to continue chatting with her, but he realized that unless he dedicated himself to his work, he'd definitely get proper punches from his chief.

They had sent texts and voicemails before but had never talked to each other. Avinash immediately called her.

'Hello,' the familiar sweet voice said.

'Hi, Alma. Birthday wishes!' Avinash gushed.

'Thank you,' the soft voice replied.

'I'm really sorry for being late. I didn't know it was your birthday when we were talking last night.'

'It's alright. We were talking for the first time, weren't we? You had no idea,' she giggled. 'It's funny.'

'I don't know why, but I'm feeling guilty for this. For wishing you this late in the day.'

'No problem. I also feel that we've known each other for a long time and that you are someone really close to me.'

'Avinaaaash!'

The young archaeologist heard his chief calling his name from a distance.

'Coming, sir.' Avinash turned back to his phone. 'Hey, listen, Alma. I've to go. I'm on duty here. How about we talk tonight after I return to my room?'

'That'll be great! Go now, go be an obedient professional.' The cute voice of Alma felt like an energy booster for Avinash.

He felt like giving her a kiss through the phone, but he was brought back to reality soon enough. Avinash had never felt so close to a girl before. For a guy who spent most of his time on books, books, and more books, this was the first time he was interacting with a girl with such enthusiasm. Sure, he had some female friends back in college, but he never communicated with them unless it was a matter of academics or profession.

Avinash sprinted to his chief. The young guy was pumped up as though he had the energy to finish the entire excavation project in that day itself. He couldn't wait to end the workday so he could go back to his room and start talking with Alma Fatima.

'Did you hear what happened nearby?' Ahmed asked. 'Some ten kilometers away from here.'

'What happened, sir?'

'Some of the mining mafia guys were found dead in a remote place. The police said they were killed by the same explosives that they were planning to use to blow up the hills,' Ahmed said with a slight hint of happiness.

'Really weird, don't you think?' Avinash scratched his beard. 'These mining mafia guys are used to these things, and all of a sudden they get killed by their own tool. Doesn't make any sense.'

'Accidents like these can happen no matter how expert you are,' Ahmed said confidently, in an ironic way. 'The Soviets accidentally blew up their nuclear reactor, didn't they? How many times did NASA's space shuttles explode, losing the lives of several astronauts? These things can happen. Human beings are so confident in their intelligence and proficiency that they think their systems are flawless.'

'Or it could be an encounter operated by the cops, made to look like an accident to save themselves from the human rights activists who always appear out of nowhere to avenge terrorists and criminals.'

'Or even that,' Ahmed grinned.

The rest of the day progressed with the usual excavation activities. With some dirt accumulated on his shirt and jeans, Avinash went back to the guesthouse and immediately called Alma Fatima.

‘Hey...birthday girl!’ Avinash beamed. ‘What was special on your birthday? Had cake? You might have had beef biryani, didn't you? Isn’t that what you people like the most?’

‘What do you mean by 'you people'?’ Alma said with a cold voice.

‘I mean Muslims. I didn't mean to stereotype you or anything. It's just that all the Muslim friends I have will go to any extent to have beef biryani. That's why I asked.’ Avinash explained, ‘I didn’t mean to offend you, sorry.’

‘I'm a vegetarian!’ Alma's reply was quick.

‘What? Wait! You got to be kidding me.’

‘It's true. I'm a vegetarian. Well, almost. I eat eggs sometimes. But I don't like meat.’ The statement was as sweet as her feminine voice.

‘Really? What happened? Somebody told you to be a vegetarian?’

‘Nobody told me anything. From an early age onwards, I hated non-veg foods. I don't know why. I never liked the taste of meat. When my parents forced me to eat, I ended up vomiting.’

‘This is really surprising,’ Avinash said with a hint of happiness. ‘Even most Hindus, whose belief system is based on non-violence and vegetarianism, gulp down meat. In Kerala, they eat beef too. It's really depressing.’

‘What about you? Aren't you a non-veg guy? Don't all Kerala guys eat meat?’

'No... nope. I'm a vegetarian too. Not even eggs,' Avinash said with pride. 'I'm also an activist in an environmental organization called EcoDot.'

'So, you're a social activist too? That's great!' Alma's clap was heard by Avinash. 'But what does vegetarianism have to do with being an environmentalist?'

'Yes, being a vegetarian is the simplest way you can fight global warming and save our planet.'

'Oh...I never knew that. How does it work?' Alma curiously asked.

'Well, livestock rearing plays a key role in the emission of greenhouse gases. It also uses up a lot more water and grains for animal rearing, which is less resourceful than using the grains for direct human consumption. Embracing vegetarianism means you can cut food-related emissions by 63 percent. About 20 percent of the methane gas emissions around the world are produced by animals raised for meat. These gases are the main cause of global warming. All combined transportation systems in the world only make up 18 percent of the emitted greenhouse gases, while animal agriculture for meat is 19 percent. Additionally, a pure vegetarian diet only needs around 1000 litres of water daily, whereas a non-veg diet needs more than 15000 litres of water per day. The non-veg diet is not efficient as well. A lot of resources, time, and energy are used for receiving something lesser. 10 kilograms of grain must be fed to cows to get 1 kilogram of meat in return. In short, an environmentalist must be a vegetarian. A meat-eating environmentalist is like a god-fearing atheist, a peace-loving terrorist, a virgin mother, and...'

'Ok...ok...I got the point.' Alma laughed. 'Gosh, you take it too far.'

'Sorry,' Avinash gushed.

'So, you're active in social work. You must be active in politics too, I assume,' Alma asked

'Nope, not in politics. But I have friends in the leadership level of some political parties.'

'Wow!' Alma exclaimed.

'Yeah, I have some friends in top universities too. If you need any help in applying for a Ph.D. or something after your post-graduation, I can help you with that.'

'That won't be necessary.' There was a certain tone of disappointment in Alma's voice.

'Oh. Are you planning to continue at the same university you're studying MA Psychology?'

'I'm sorry. I lied,' Alma sobbed.

'What happened? What is it?'

'I dropped my post-graduation studies a few months ago. My parents want me to get married and be a housewife,' Alma said, her voice had a dismal chill.

'You want that?' Avinash asked curiously.

'Of course not, I want to continue my studies but my parents won't let me. They already fixed a guy, Ashraf, to marry me.'

'Oh...so you're engaged?' Avinash asked. His voice was virtually silent.

'No. Not yet. I haven't seen or talked to that guy yet.'

'Do you know what happens when you marry him? Any plans?'

'The usual things. I'll have to serve him for the rest of my life without leaving the boundaries of home.'

'Don't you want to escape that fate?' Avinash asked.

'I need to...' Alma sighed. 'But how?'

'Marry a guy who will support your education and career,' Avinash consoled.

'I don't think I will get any such guy to marry me,' Alma replied, with a sound of hopelessness but still with some hints of hope in it.

Avinash opened his mouth to say something but then closed it.

'Why aren't you saying anything?' Alma asked.

'Don't worry, Alma. You'll get someone who will understand you and support you all the way,' Avinash soothed her.

# 06

'Good evening, and welcome to NewsTonight,' the popular host of the regional TV news network announced on his live show. 'Today, the union government passed a bill in parliament enacting a new law that prohibits the distribution, sale, or consumption of beef. This Act is undoubtedly a significant blow to a vast portion of the country's population. Millions of people in this nation rely on beef as their primary diet, and the union government has shown no sympathy toward them. Is this the first step in the national government's attempt to turn the nation into a primarily Hindu-fundamentalist state? Let's debate. Tonight, we have Adv. Padmaraj from the Nationalist Party and Mr. Riaz from the Conference Party joining us in the news studio. We also have Mr. Ragesh Nakutty from the Leftist Party joining us from the Capital studio to discuss this latest development. First, let's turn to Adv. Padmaraj.'

The screen now displayed two boxes: one with the host and the other with Padmaraj. 'Adv. Padmaraj, what explanation can you give about this insensitive law enacted by your party ruling at the centre?'

'You've got it all wrong. How can you spread false news on such a prime-time live program?' Adv. Padmaraj snapped.

'No need for accusations, Adv. Padmaraj. It is the last resort of those who don't have any explanations for their wrong deeds,' the host said calmly, as if calming someone.

'I'll make everything clear. This act doesn't ban beef distribution or consumption. I'll repeat, this act doesn't ban beef distribution or consumption. It is merely a law to regulate the beef industry to standardize it,' Adv. Padmaraj emphasized each word.

'You're not explaining anything, Adv. Padmaraj. You are simply wasting our time. I now turn to Mr. Riaz—'

'Wait a minute... I haven't finished. Let me explain,' Padmaraj struggled.

'I'll give you another chance later. Now, on to Mr. Riaz. How do you perceive this new law? How will it affect the large portion of the population dependent on beef?' The host was still visible on one side of the screen, while the box on the other side now showed Riaz instead of Padmaraj.

'This is entirely a barbaric law. Nothing more can be said about it. How can a government dictate the diet of the people? The government should be concerned about feeding its citizens, not taking food away from them. Honestly, this is not a shock to me. I'm not shocked. I always expected this kind of attitude from the central government. Their intentions are dire,' Riaz said furiously.

'Mr. Ragesh, what is your opinion about this new law? You have always been a fiery critic of the Nationalist Party, which rules the centre. Tell us, the viewers want to know the Leftist Party's stand on this subject.'

'Today, the fascist party ruling at the centre has revealed its true face. Their new law is preposterous, vicious, and atrocious. They have taken away the basic right to food. Millions of people depend on beef for their livelihood. Tens of thousands of poor Indians' only source of income is from the beef business. Beef also holds historical and cultural significance for certain people in India. By banning beef, the fascist central government aims to erase the existence of these people. The extreme-right Nationalist Party is trying to establish their jingoist nation, and banning beef is the first step. It is a fundamental right to choose what to eat. No government has any say in it. I assure you, in the state of Kerala where the Leftist Party is in power, there will be beef available at any time, regardless of the laws made by the fascists at the centre. You know why the Nationalist Party introduced such a law? Is it because they love animals? Is it because they want to create a meatless environment? No! It's because the activists of this Nationalist Party are communal and extremely religious people. They base their lives on Hinduism and want to turn this nation into a Hindu-extremist one. As we all know, Hinduism is about vegetarianism, and they consider cows as mothers. How can someone consider an animal as a mother? This is barbaric and primitive. Today they banned beef. Tomorrow they will ban chicken, and soon we can expect a law that will ban all non-vegetarian food. The central government has proven to be authoritarian and undemocratic. It is high time we overthrow this government and establish a new, deserving one.'

'Now, it is time for a break,' the host said, looking straight at the camera.

Although viewers at home could only see commercials, another conversation was happening in the studio.

'This is really unfair,' Padmaraj sighed to the host. 'You didn't even give me enough time to explain. You cut me off in the middle of my time while you allotted ample time for the others. If you plan to lead this discussion in such a manner, I have no option but to leave.'

'In that case, I will announce to our viewers that you left because you couldn't find answers to the accusations,' the host replied.

Adv. Padmaraj couldn't breathe or say anything. He just sat silently for a few seconds.

'Alright, but I request you to give me time to explain. Don't cut me off when I'm speaking,' he said.

'I can't guarantee that,' the host replied flatly. 'I'm the moderator of this debate, and if I find you beating around the bush without coming to the point, I have no option but to turn to other panellists. This is a valuable prime-time spot. We can't waste time here.'

Padmaraj didn't reply to this.

'Welcome back to NewsTonight,' the host announced to the camera. 'Now we go to the spokesperson of the Nationalist

Party. Tell us, Adv. Padmaraj, can the decision made by the central government be justified?'

'As the viewers are my witness, I request enough time to explain,' Padmaraj cleared his throat. 'You all have completely misinterpreted the new act. First, I must start with the basics. The other panel members have accused this act of being undemocratic and our government of being fascist. I remind you that the bill was introduced in both houses of parliament. After scrutiny, it was passed by the majority of parliament members in a highly democratic way. How can such an act be called undemocratic?'

'Adv. Padmaraj, we don't want to hear about the parliamentary procedures. Tell us about the law. That's what we want to hear,' the host said irritably.

'How can I move forward without clarifying the baseless allegations?' Padmaraj growled. 'Now, onto the law. This isn't new. Cow slaughter has always been illegal in India since time immemorial. In ancient and medieval times, killing a cow was punishable by death. After India became a republic, about six states made any kind of beef completely illegal, while nine states made cow slaughter illegal. Nevertheless, the current law we're discussing doesn't ban beef totally. This law makes a certain form of beef processing illegal. I will elabourate.'

'And please do that quickly,' the host chipped in.

'Yes. Most beef manufacturing in the country is done in an unhygienic and destructive way. Although the beef industry itself is harmful to nature and contributes significantly to global warming, we aim to control it by legalizing those manufacturers willing to continue their business under the standards set by the food authority. Currently, cattle are killed by slitting their throats with blunt knives, causing them to suffer and bleed to death. In some places, they are slaughtered by hammering their heads. These primitive practices can't be tolerated in such a civilized nation. Therefore, the current law regulates how beef is manufactured. Consumers will continue to get beef from legal suppliers.'

'Who do you think we are, Mr. Padmaraj?' Ragesh bellowed. 'Do you think we are fools? We aren't satisfied with your explanation! I will personally lead protests against this law from tomorrow. Your fascist government will fall!'

The NewsTonight program ended on a bitter note, as always. Amidst all this, Ragesh was content with the latest development. He called for a meeting with his close comrades and was busy organizing a protest for the next day.

It was particularly busy at Kavadi Junction in the city. The time was around 8:45 am, and the street was crowded with commuters and pedestrians. There wasn't any space left on the road for a vehicle to park, yet a pickup truck found a way to place itself conveniently, making it visible to anyone in the area. Out of nowhere, about two dozen men assembled around it with red flags. Among them, Comrade Ragesh heroically appeared with a microphone in hand. The driver of the pickup truck went to the back and opened the cargo door, revealing a calf lying on the bed.

'My dear comrades,' Ragesh announced through his

microphone, 'if we don't protest now, it will be too late. As you all are aware, the fascist government at the centre has passed a law making beef distribution and consumption illegal. My friends, this is a violation of your freedom. They are taking away your fundamental rights. It is our duty to protest against this barbaric law.'

All the comrades present clapped. Kavadi Junction witnessed a sudden traffic jam as the pickup truck and all those comrades occupied half of the road during the morning rush hour. There was a school bus directly beside the pickup truck, unable to move forward because of the jam. The kids in the school bus curiously watched the unfolding event.

'Today, I want to prove to you all that you can eat whatever you want. No matter what laws they make, those fascists can't stop us. I will prove that to you. Let's see if they can stop me!' Ragesh handed the microphone to a comrade and climbed to the back of the pickup truck. Seeing him, the cow stood up. A comrade passed a blunt knife to Ragesh. Three other comrades also clambered in and made sure the calf was tightly bound.

The unsuspecting people of the street froze, watching the event unfold. The kids in the school bus had no idea what they were about to witness.

Comrade Ragesh Nakutty gripped the calf's head with one hand and began to incise its neck from one end. Blood dripped out, splattering on the clean shirts of the comrades. The blunt knife got stuck in the calf's thick skin. The calf shook violently but couldn't move its legs. Its head was held firmly by another comrade. Ragesh sliced away, cutting some muscle parts of the calf. He then inserted the knife into the wide-open slot of the calf's neck and, with maximum effort, finally managed to slit its throat. It took another couple of minutes for the calf to die completely. Blood poured from the pickup truck like a waterfall. All the comrades clapped and chanted, 'Long Live Revolution! Long Live Revolution!'

Comrade Ragesh jumped off the truck and took the microphone again. 'Dear all, I request you not to leave. You can participate in this protest against the central government's barbaric law by joining our Beef Festival shortly. The meat from this calf will be used to prepare the beef. Our comrades are setting up a pavilion to cook the beef to be served to you all. Please stay or come back at 12 pm. We will be waiting for you. Long Live Revolution! Down with the Barbaric Anti-Beef Law!'

As the comrades went to the side of the road to set up the pavilion on the footpath and the truck left, the road became free for commuters. The traffic jam eased, but there was still considerable rush. The comrades erected the pavilion within half an hour. A cooking gas cylinder, stove, and other necessary utensils were brought to the spot. The calf was skinned and butchered by professionals, who were likely not comrades. The flesh was cut, chopped, and garnished with spices.

As promised by Comrade Ragesh, the beef was ready by 12 pm. All the comrades were shouting slogans. On non-degradable plates, the beef was served to the comrades. Comrade Ragesh was noticeably happy. He invited passing pedestrians to have the dish, and some comrades stopped passing motorcyclists to serve them beef.

The event was covered and broadcasted by news channels. Ragesh gave interviews about the necessity of eating beef and protesting the barbaric law of the central government. That night, Comrade Ragesh and his friends celebrated at their party house.

'Today's protest was a success. Every news channel covered it, and we are in the positive limelight again,' Ragesh said to a senior party leader.

Their talk went on for another hour, but then one comrade's face fell as he scrolled through Facebook on his phone.

'Comrade,' the comrade said in a mild voice, 'we are being heavily criticized on social media.'

'What do you mean?' Ragesh's smile faded.

'An article against us has gone viral,' the comrade showed the phone to Ragesh. 'It says here that Ragesh, who organized the beef festival today, should first feed the starving tribal people of his former constituency. Hundreds of children from the region where Ragesh represented in parliament for ten years are dying of malnutrition. Ragesh, who is so enthusiastic about serving people beef, should go and serve these children some basic grains.'

Ragesh's eyebrows furrowed. 'Who wrote this article?'

'Someone named Avinash Mahadevan.'

# 07

A car with an emblem of the central government had to stop in front of the gate as a couple of security personnel asked them to halt for checks.

'We're from the central government,' the driver said to the security guy. 'On government duty. Let us pass.'

The other security guy, who appeared to be not as clueless as his colleague, asked, 'Sir, we didn't get any intimation. Therefore, I'm afraid I have to disturb you further by asking for more details. Just tell me the name of the officer and the purpose of the visit. I'll write it down in the register, and then I can open the gates for you.'

The tinted glass of the back door of the car slowly rolled down to reveal a man in his late forties wearing sunglasses.

'Hey, kindly open the gate. I don't have time for chit-chat. I want to make sure whether you and your company can keep working in the coming days,' the man said without any particular tone.

Alarmed, the two security personnel opened the automated gate with a press of a red button. The car went in and stopped at the entrance to the main office.

The officer, with frameless spectacles and a thick moustache, walked right in with his assistant, a young thin guy in his mid-20s. The officer stopped at the security guard at the door, not to ask for permission to enter but to order him to lead him to the manager in charge of the chemical factory they were in.

The chubby manager was sitting in his office with his legs on the table. He dropped his legs to the floor and stood up as he saw the officer and his assistant coming in.

'I'm Suresh Tiwari, Special Officer, Pollution Violations Department, Ministry of Environment and Climate Change. I'm here for an inspection,' the officer stated on his way toward the manager to shake hands.

'Sir...if you had informed us earlier, we would've made the arrangements,' the manager stammered.

'What arrangements?' Suresh Tiwari smirked. 'I'm not here for biryani.'

'Sir, please sit down. Do you prefer tea or coffee? Sugar or without?' the manager asked politely.

'None. I just want to finish what I've come here for.' Suresh was still standing.

The manager was sweating all over. He escorted Suresh and his assistant to the control room of the factory. It was a room with consoles and screens on all sides, leaving just the area around the door alone. Anyone in the control room could watch most of the factory through the glass pane in front of them. Other areas could be watched through the screens set above, which had inputs from the factory's CCTV cameras.

'Bring me today's attendance register for all the departments,' Suresh ordered the manager.

The manager called the labour officer of the factory and passed the order.

Suresh Tiwari scanned through the CCTV monitors until the attendance register came. He sat down and started reading it.

'Over fifty employees are absent for the past few months. Why is that?' Suresh asked, and before the manager could open his mouth, he added, 'Please don't waste my time lying that all those were just taking leaves. Tell the truth.'

'They don't work here anymore, sir,' the manager sputtered.

'Then why are their names in the register?'

The manager kept his mouth shut, only shivering his lips.

'I'll answer that for you.' Suresh leered. 'These are essential positions mandatory in any chemical factory as set by the law of the government. The employees in these positions check pollution control and related environmental aspects of the factory. They prevent possible leakages, control toxic effluents from being dumped into the rivers, and look after labour safety as well. However, I assume the management of this factory recognized these employees as trivial and a waste of money to spend on monthly salaries. Therefore, they were fired gradually. Yet, the names are kept in the register so that the government wouldn't know about it. But you guys couldn't fill it up with fake signs not expecting me to come on such short notice. Tell me, am I wrong?'

The manager didn't answer.

'I take that as a no. I'm right, aren't I?' Suresh said. 'Now, give me a tour of your facility.'

Suresh Tiwari and his assistant were led by the manager and the labour officer to the factory floor. Suresh asked his assistant to take pictures of whatever he pointed at.

'Look at that...a rusty edge...a broken conveyor belt...a broken pipe...a degrading wall...a leaking sewage...Faulty wires...'

The assistant found himself busy noting down every problem of the factory. The shrewd eyes of Suresh Tiwari captured every fault of every inch. The manager and the labour officer were trembling with fear.

'Now let's go back to the office,' Suresh said to the manager.

This time, Suresh Tiwari and his assistant sat in chairs inside the manager's office. The labour officer was also present in the room.

'Do you know why I came here?' Suresh asked the manager.

'Usual checking, isn't it, sir?' the manager stammered.

'No, it's not,' Suresh said. 'The fish population in the local river has plummeted. The State Pollution Control Board was proven ineffective in handling these situations. The natives directly approached us. My team tested the sample from the river and it was found to be highly toxic. Our team also found that your factory has been dumping untreated effluents into the river. I came here to check the functioning of this factory. How could you miss properly treating the sewage before dumping it into freshwater? Now I understand, you guys have fired all employees who could've saved the environment and even sold off the equipment capable of doing the same.'

The manager kept his silence. His eyes wandered off to the corner of the room.

'I have pretty bad news that you have to pass to your management. Anyhow, we will also officially do that from our end as well,' Suresh said flatly.

Suresh extended his arm to his assistant, and the young man handed over a document. Suresh signed at the bottom of the paper and took it.

'I want to let you know that your factory is hereby-'

A sudden scream of alarming sirens interrupted Suresh Tiwari. The whole factory premises were immersed in the noise of the siren.

'What is it?' Suresh asked.

'Malfunctioning. But the factory has stopped all operations. I don't know what happened,' the manager said.

They all went out from the office, and a middle-aged man with a tag 'supervisor' was sprinting towards them.

'What happened?' the manager asked.

'The factory has been shut down due to technical problems,' the supervisor panted.

'What is it?'

'It appears the pipe that carries the waste to the river is blocked, and all those effluents are rushing back to the factory,' the supervisor said.

'What? That's absurd. The pipes are big enough for a person to crawl through,' the manager said.

'I don't know. We need to check it,' the supervisor said. 'Until then, the factory is temporarily shut down.'

'Okay. Let's go,' the manager said.

'I'm coming with you,' added Suresh Tiwari.

The government car and the factory's four-wheel-drive jeep dashed through the western Indian terrain until they reached the marshes. The tarred road diverted in another direction. Both cars stopped at the curve.

The manager got off the jeep and approached the car.

'Sir, your car won't be able to drive through this terrain. You have to come with us in the jeep,' the manager said.

Suresh Tiwari and his assistant got off from their car and entered the factory's jeep. They sat in the back with the supervisor while the manager was in the front alongside the driver. The jeep entered the mushy terrain and trudged carefully. Suresh could hear the mud splashing and splitting across. The marshy land was visible all around. It was so eerie that if a dead body were dumped here, it couldn't be discovered even if the earth ran dry.

They drove for ten minutes. Suresh felt as though he was part of a juggling session. Sometimes the jeep got stuck in one place and it took a good effort from the driver to push it through, burning a lot of fuel. Finally, the gigantic pipe was visible. It came out of nowhere parallel to them, through the marshes and it was disappearing into the distance as well.

'Where do you think the pipe is blocked?' Suresh asked the supervisor who was sitting opposite him.

'We've calculated the pressure and other factors. It's somewhere nearby.'

'Stop! Stop!' the manager said.

The jeep stopped and everyone got off. Suresh's assistant was a bit irritated by the fact that he stepped on mud, which ruined his clean trousers.

'There it is...' the supervisor said.

'What the...?' the manager was in all awe.

'Can't we move closer?' Suresh asked.

'No, we can't. We'll drown,' the driver replied.

'But what in the world happened to this?' the manager's mouth was wide open as though a train could pass through it.

The sight was extraordinary. The giant iron pipe was fractured at one point. From that point onwards, it was crushed in the marshes, immersed deep beyond visibility. The other part was twisted, curved, and what seemed to be a knot made with the iron pipe as though it was just a thin thread. Thick vines were all around the pipe. It was covered almost fully by them.

'Do you think some environmental activist group did this?' the manager asked.

'This is something even Superman couldn't do!' Suresh Tiwari replied.

The manager took out his phone and began calling his superiors. He was frantic and apparently didn't know how to react.

Suresh Tiwari saw his assistant as awestruck as he was.

'Sir, is there any explanation for all this?' the assistant asked.

'I don't know, boy. I'd be more than happy if you could come up with anything.'

Somehow, the news got leaked. Consequently, the incident garnered wide media attention. A couple of news teams came to the place by night, but they couldn't even see the scene for themselves because of the darkness. They returned to their offices and came back early in the morning even before sunrise. This time, there were around a dozen news groups. All from print and TV. The cameras were busy recording the weird configuration of the giant pipes. The news reports didn't further need any more time to spread across other media. Social media platforms were filled with this incident. All of them had their own theories. Some reported that it was the work of some environmental activist groups, which was obviously alleged by the factory management. While some claimed that this is the result of an unknown natural phenomenon like an earthquake. Others suspected extra-terrestrial aliens being responsible for all this.

Suresh Tiwari was reading such an article on his smartphone. He was on his way to his hometown on a train. There wasn't an airport near his hometown, therefore he needed to travel by rail to reach there from his office. The journey would usually take seven hours if it was a super-fast train. The railway track stretched across the woods, which was considerably an uninhabited area.

Although entertaining, all those crazy speculations about the incident he himself witnessed made him sleepy. Suresh dozed off as soon as he put the smartphone back in his pocket. He expected to cover another sixty kilometres by the time he woke up.

However, when Suresh woke up, he saw the train had stopped.

'How long has this train been stopped?' he asked a fellow passenger.

'For the past half hour,' he replied.

'Perhaps it's halted for the next station to be cleared off by the previous train,' another passenger said.

All the passengers inside the compartment waited for another twenty minutes until they became restless.

'I'm going out to check,' one of them said.

Coincidentally, it was the same time most other passengers got off the train to try to identify the reason behind this unusual stoppage.

Yet another fifteen minutes passed.

The passenger from Suresh's compartment who went outside came back.

'You will not believe this!' the man was hysterical.

'What is it?' a fellow passenger asked.

'You won't believe me if I tell you,' the man said. 'You have to go look for yourself.'

'What if the train starts when we are out?' another passenger asked.

'Nope, the train is not going anywhere for a few days,' the man said, sweating.

Everyone got off the train, including Suresh Tiwari.

He saw hundreds of passengers in front of him walking forward. They were all murmuring to each other. Suresh Tiwari shouldered through to the front. It was difficult to see what was happening because of the crowd. Yet, Suresh managed to come up front and got a clear view.

Around 200 meters away, the railway track had literally vanished into the ground. From his position itself, the tracks were covered with vines and thick roots. The vines got dense progressively, and at 200 meters away, probably with the force or by the weight of the vines and roots, the railway track had drowned into the ground, gradually disappearing into the rocks and finally immersed into the ground. Totally vanished, unable to carry any train forward. Fortunately, the locomotive driver anticipated the danger as soon as the track was covered and coiled by thin vines a kilometre before. He was able to drag the train to a complete stop, avoiding a major disaster.

Everyone was busy taking photos of the phenomenon as it was a once-in-a-lifetime sight for them.

Whereas Suresh Tiwari left the crowd and was concerned about something worse.

'So, tomorrow is my last day here,' Avinash said to Alma on the phone while lying on the bed.

'Yeah, I remember you told me that before,' Alma replied. 'You know, I was actually counting the days... for you to return.'

'Really?'

'Well, yeah... Did you have dinner?'

'I did. How about you?'

'Yep.'

'And...?'

'Hmm...'

'So...?'

'What's up?'

'So, tomorrow is the last day of excavation here. We're

leaving the day after tomorrow.'

'You said that a while ago.'

'Oh...'

'Hmmm...'

'You had dinner?'

'Yes, and you?'

'I did. I told you before...'

'Hmmm...'

'So... I'll let you sleep now. Finish off your work tomorrow and return,' Alma said. 'I can't wait to see you.'

'Me too.'

Avinash placed his phone beside him and closed his eyes to sleep. No matter how hard he tried, he couldn't manage to doze off. He checked his phone multiple times. There were no notifications. Thirty minutes passed. Avinash grabbed his phone and texted Alma.

'Hey, I want to tell you something.'

Alma was offline, but the message was delivered. The grey double ticks turned blue in front of Avinash.

'Yeah... tell me,' Alma replied.

'Well...' Avinash typed and sent.

'Tell me...' Alma responded.

'Good night,' Avinash sent the message. 'See you tomorrow.'

Avinash saw Alma typing something, but then she only sent a smile emoji. He put the phone beside him and tried to sleep again. After five minutes, he took the phone and dialled Alma.

'Hey!' she answered.

'Hi,' Avinash greeted. 'So... not sleepy?'

'I love you,' Avinash said suddenly.

There was complete silence. Avinash could hear nothing from the other end of the phone.

'Alma...?' he called.

Still no reply.

'I'm sorry,' Avinash said and hung up the call. He lay back, looking at the ceiling fan. A minute passed, and he heard his phone vibrating. He picked it up.

'Why did you hang up?' Alma said.

'I thought you were angry,' Avinash replied.

'What made you think that?'

'You didn't reply.'

'I was overwhelmed that I couldn't even breathe properly.'

'I'm sorry, Alma,' Avinash said. 'Please forget what happened.'

'What if I don't want to forget?' Alma asked sweetly. 'What if I want that again?'

'What?'

'The thing you said to me?'

'Which one?'

'The three words.'

'I love you?'

'I love you too.'

'What?'

'What what?'

'Say that again,' Avinash said quickly.

'I love you too,' Alma replied.

'Ouch!'

'What happened?' Alma asked.

'Nothing... I just pinched myself to check if this was a dream!'

'Silly you,' Alma laughed.

'Tell me...'

'There's nothing more to talk about,' Alma said firmly. 'You go to sleep, young man. You have work tomorrow.'

'But I want to tell you...'

'Hey!' Alma interjected. 'You finish your work tomorrow. Come back home. We'll see each other, and you have your whole life in front of you to tell me whatever you want, okay?'

'Okay!'

‘Then, good night. Sleep tight,’ Alma said softly.

‘Good night, Alma,’ Avinash replied and tucked himself in to sleep.

After recording the weight of the final artefact on the list, Avinash gave the document to Prof. Ahmed for his authorizing signature.

‘So, what are your plans after this?’ Ahmed asked after signing the document and putting it aside.

‘Well, I've got about a month before going back to the university,’ Avinash said. ‘I have some activities with EcoDot.’

‘Oh... that environmental organization you're part of?’ Ahmed walked towards him. ‘But aren't you going to spend time with your parents?’

‘They're living in a town far away from the city I live in. I'll visit them when I get time. But first, I've got to do those EcoDot duties.’

‘When was the last time you saw your parents?’ Ahmed asked.

‘Hmm... I think... maybe about two years ago,’ Avinash replied, noticing the disappointment on Ahmed's face. ‘I was traveling, as you know.’

‘Don't forget to take care of your parents,’ Ahmed said and walked away without waiting for a reply.

The archaeologists checked whether all the excavated artefacts were sealed. They ran over the list again and supervised the items being packed and transported to the ASI office. The local labourers bid farewell to the archaeology team, visibly sad. After having a cup of refreshing tea at the site, the archaeologists got into the government-sponsored vehicle and left for their bungalow.

Avinash took his already packed bag and left for the railway station. Prof. Ahmed had his train the next day, so he stayed back at the guest house.

'Attention passengers!' the announcement let Avinash know that his train would be four hours late.

He sat back in the uncomfortable seat of the railway station. He had always wondered why the seats at Indian railway stations were so uncomfortable. Either you'd end up with back pain or you'd just slide off to the ground.

'It's to prevent people from spending too much time in the railway station and making it their home,' Alma had explained.

'Oh... that makes sense,' Avinash said. 'Why didn't I come up with that explanation?'

'It's done intentionally. It's called hostile architecture,' Alma had started to lecture. 'Homeless people tend to stay longer or sleep in such public places. That's why.'

'Yes, I understand,' Avinash had replied, feeling disappointed.

'What happened?' Alma had asked.

'No, I have this feeling,' Avinash had said. 'What if Mother Nature gets the same idea and starts being hostile to us? We humans are exploiting her a lot.'

'Crazy idea,' Alma had laughed. 'Mother Nature gets mad once in a while. We witness earthquakes, tsunamis, and stuff like that, don't we?'

'Hmm...'

'Hey, tell me, what are your plans when you reach home?'

'Meeting you, of course.'

'No. You said something about your environmental activities.'

'It can wait.'

'No, it can't. You planned it before. So, finish that stuff first. I'll wait. Just tell me when you will be free after that.'

'It'll take some three or four days. I just have to organize some protests and prepare some action plans. After that, I'll come meet you.'

'Aren't you going to visit your parents and spend time with them?' Alma asked with concern. 'After all, it's been a long time since you saw them.'

'Is it necessary? They can look after themselves.'

'Don't you have a sense of responsibility? Aren't your old parents living alone? Go meet them and make arrangements to take care of them.'

'What do all these have to do with you?' Avinash had replied roughly.

'Have some commitment to the people who raised you. You

preach about Mother Nature and protecting the environment so much. Why can't you take care of your real mother and father? If you fail to do so, how can I trust you to take care of me?'

Avinash had stayed silent.

'Don't you have anything to say?' Alma had shouted softly, which Avinash had never known was possible. 'I'll come to meet you only if you go to your parents and spend some time with them.'

'Okay!' he had replied.

'What ok?'

'Okay... I agree with everything you said.'

'Really?'

'Yes. Honestly.'

'So, what are your plans?'

'Reach Kerala. EcoDot works. Visit my parents. Spend some days there with them. Then you,' Avinash had said like a school kid answering his teacher.

'Good boy!'

Avinash had realized that he was on the edge of the metallic seat, slowly sliding away unknowingly. He pulled himself back.

'This should be a mutual thing,' Avinash had said.

'What?'

'Ordering things to do.'

'Okay. Tell me what you want me to do,' Alma had asked. Avinash could hear her blinking.

'Continue your studies. Pursue post-graduation. Do a PhD. Get a job,' Avinash had said firmly.

'I told you. My folks won't allow. They want me to marry right now,' Alma had cried.

'We'll marry. The day after our marriage, you'll resume your studies. Fine?'

'Do you think our marriage is going to be easy?' Alma had said. 'We belong to different religions.'

'Hmm...'

'I hope you have some plan?'

'Honestly, I don't. Well, we won't face any problems from my side. What about yours?'

'Conservative Islamic family,' Alma had said. 'They will only let me marry a Muslim guy.'

'What will we do?'

'I thought you would come up with some idea.'

'We'll worry about that later. When the time comes, things will fall into place.'

'The time when my family forces me into a marriage with another guy?'

'No, we'll sort this out before that. Don't worry.'

‘After marriage, will you let me join your environmental activities?’

Avinash had pulled himself back to the seat after realizing that he was almost on the ground.

‘There's no need for permission. You should work with me for the cause,’ Avinash had said while looking at the digital clock on the railway station. There was still one more hour for the train to arrive.

‘Tell me, what are the tasks at hand for your organization?’ Alma had asked.

‘EcoDot is involved in many activities for environmental protection. I am charged with some issues in Kerala. Usually, like any other environmental organization, they focus on anti-plastic activities. This involves spreading awareness of the damages caused by plastics and distributing plastic alternative products. However, personally, I started an anti-non-vegetarian program for EcoDot. They aren't very keen on that.’

‘Why is that?’

‘As I said last time, most environmentalists are non-vegetarians. The meat industry causes pollution and speeds up global warming.’

‘Why didn't you explain that to them?’

‘They aren't listening. EcoDot doesn't transfer funds for this activity. As a result, I'm raising money on my own.’

‘Really? Where do you get the money from?’ Avinash heard the call getting hung up by Alma.

He didn't call back as he knew why it had happened. He stared at the railway track and then at the clock. The platform echoed with the announcement that the train would arrive shortly.

Avinash took his metallic water bottle and filled it with drinking water available on the railway station platform. He came back and sat on the uncomfortable chair. It was particularly cold that night.

An old man sat next to him.

'The train is late, isn't it?' the old man asked Avinash.

'Yes, it is.'

'Do you know why?' the man took off his spectacles and slowly wiped them clean.

'Isn't this usual?'

'No, it isn't. Trains aren't usually late around here,' he wore the specs back on his nose.

'Then what is it?'

'Some railway tracks in the country are mysteriously disappearing into the ground.'

'What do you mean?'

'Yes, it was in the news. Some tracks are completely useless now. So, the railway management has to reschedule and manage the trains. It's chaos. Consequently, every train is late.'

'Disappearing?' Avinash stared at the man. 'I don't understand.'

‘Neither does anyone, my boy,’ the old man laughed.

Avinash's phone rang. It was Alma.

‘Hey... sorry. My mom just came into the room,’ she said modestly.

‘It's okay,’ Avinash said. ‘Alma, do you watch the news?’

‘I don't have that habit.’

‘I heard something about railway tracks disappearing. Just wanted to know if it was in the news.’

‘In which world are you living? Don't you have the internet on your phone? Just search for that news,’ Alma giggled. ‘We aren't living in ancient times, are we?’

‘Oh, I forgot about that,’ Avinash laughed. ‘But just imagine, what if one fine day, we wake up to find a world without the internet or any other telecommunication.’

‘Don't want to imagine that. I have enough troubles already.’

‘A world without radiation, a world without plastics, a world without pollution-’

‘A world without trains, and you would have to walk home unless you can afford a horse,’ Alma laughed so hard that her mother opened the door.

Avinash could hear Alma's mother asking why she was laughing, and Alma replied that it was because of some meme. The phone was hung up soon after.

The train arrived, and Avinash boarded.

Hope the track home isn't missing yet.

O.0Fully loaded, twelve garbage trucks arrived at the gates of the Brahmanagar landfill. The gates were opened by the security guard.

'I don't think there is much space here anymore,' said the security guard.

'Where should I dump the waste then?' asked Satish, the driver of the first truck.

'I was just saying. See if you can find a spot,' replied the security guard.

'When will your manager come? We have to report this,' said the driver.

'He'll come at 11. Just go to the office after this.'

The twelve garbage trucks split up to find a spot to dump with the help of other Municipal Corporation employees. It seemed as though the dump yard would rival the heights of the Himalayas any day soon. The Municipal Corporation of the city in the state of Kerala is ruled by the same political party as the state government. Most of the staff were appointed by the Leftist party as well.

The landfill staff somehow managed to accommodate the newly arrived garbage. Concerned, Satish and a few other staff members went to the office where Babu, the manager, was checking some documents.

'Sir, you have to do something about the space here,' requested Satish.

'I'm very well aware of that fact, but what can I do?' Babu seemed helpless.

'You're the manager here. Tell the garbage recycling company to clear this mess up,' Satish said.

'What garbage recycling company?' wondered Babu.

'You genuinely don't know?' asked one of the staff.

Babu looked at all of them.

'Yeah, right. I just didn't know you were talking about that. Yeah, yeah. K-Kare Limited,' said Babu.

Then there were a few seconds of awkward silence.

'Well?' asked Satish.

'What?' said Babu, still in confusion.

'Call them now,' said Satish. 'I saw in the news that the company was paid 60 crores by the Municipal Corporation for this cleanup job. I also heard that when Andami Company gave a quote for just 10 crores, it was overlooked in favour of K-Kare Limited.'

'Hey, Satish. It seems like you're following some right-wing news portals. K-Kare Limited is the suitable company for this job. It is a huge multinational company with branches all across the globe. They have immense experience in recycling and taking care of trash. Whereas, this Andami Company belongs to this capitalist Andami of Gujarat who has leanings with the central government. If they are given a minute space here, these capitalists will exploit proletarians like you and start intervening in other matters of the city,' stated Babu.

'I'm a poor proletarian, like you said. I don't have much knowledge of any multinational company or any from Gujarat. Just call whoever is responsible and save us from this mess,' said Satish dramatically.

'Alright. I'll call them. But as it is a big multinational company, it will take time to get connected with the right staff. As I heard lately, they are currently dealing with some 500 crore clean-up project of the Turkish earthquake,' replied Babu.

'We're going. Our shift is over. Just make sure things are running properly,' said Satish, turning around and walking away.

Babu dialled the contact number of K-Kare Limited. In the same city, the phone rang. There was no one near the phone. The phone was accompanied by the table it rested upon and the plastic chair in front of it. There were some visiting cards and a brochure of Human Chain against the Centre's Fascist Policies on the table. It was a single room. Not even a toilet was attached to it. The phone's ring could be heard by the people of the neighbouring shop, which sold lottery tickets. It was a shopping centre with multiple shops. The K-Kare office was the odd one that was locked.

'That's strange,' said a staff member of the lottery shop. 'That office usually never gets any calls. Wonder who is calling there.'

A customer of the lottery shop stretched to see the locked office with a small board, K-Kare Pvt. Ltd., above the door.

'What kind of office is this?' asked the customer.

'I literally have no idea. One young guy comes in the morning, spends half an hour there, and leaves. He comes again in the evening and leaves after five minutes,' replied the lottery guy.

The phone rang again, but there was no one to pick up the call.

By evening, a young guy came to the office, scrolling through Facebook on his phone.

'Boy, the phone was ringing in your office since morning. Call them back,' said the lottery guy.

'It's a landline. There isn't any call identifier to know which number the call came from,' replied the boy.

The young guy opened the lock and went in. He signed an attendance register and was about to leave. The phone stayed silent.

The guy closed the door and was busy locking it when he

heard a vibration on his cell phone. He took it out to find a meme being forwarded to his WhatsApp by some random person. He found it amusing and was about to reply when he heard the phone in the office ring again. He acted as though he didn't hear the ring and continued to leave.

'Hey, boy, your office phone is ringing. Go pick it up,' said the lottery shop staff.

'Why are you bothering me, old man,' replied the young guy.

'At least show some commitment to the job you're getting paid for, son,' said the lottery shop staff.

The young guy's face revealed a sense of irritation. He slowly walked back to the office to open the door. It seemed as though he purposefully did so to make the ring die out. As he expected, the phone hung up when he opened the door. He turned around and smiled at the lottery staff and proceeded to close the door. However, the phone rang again. The young guy looked at the lottery shop staff helplessly. He smiled back at the young guy. Reluctantly, the young guy opened the door again and picked up the call.

'Hello!' said the young guy with as little energy as possible.

'K-Kare office?' asked Babu.

'Yes,' replied the young guy.

'I'm Babu calling from Brahmanagar landfill,' said Babu. 'You guys need to do something about the garbage.'

'What should I do?' asked the young guy.

Babu didn't have an answer for that.

‘Can I know who I’m speaking to?’ asked Babu.

‘I’m the operations officer,’ replied the young guy.

‘So…Mr. Operations Officer, what are we supposed to do with the garbage problem at Brahmanagar? K-Kare has the responsibility to clear it,’ said Babu.

‘I don’t know,’ replied the young guy.

Babu stayed silent again.

‘Who runs the company?’ asked Babu.

‘I don’t know,’ said the young guy.

‘Who appointed you?’ asked Babu, frustrated.

‘That’s Mr. Raghunath,’ replied the young guy.

‘Raghunath? The former District Secretary of the party?’

‘Yeah,’ confirmed the young guy.

‘So, you were an SFY activist?’ asked Babu.

‘Not just an activist. I was the Arts Club Secretary of Maharani College.’

‘Can you give me the number of Raghunath?’

‘Just hold on for a minute,’ the young guy was scrolling through his cell phone. ‘Here you go, it is 8 -5…’

Babu wrote it down in his office and hung up the call as soon as he confirmed that there were ten digits to it. He immediately dialled Raghunath.

‘Mr. Raghunath, I’m calling from Brahmanagar landfill,’ he said in a rush.

'Yes, tell me,' replied the rough voice.

'K-Kare company needs to look into the problem of the garbage here,' said Babu.

'It will be taken care of,' said Raghunath.

'It's an emergency. There isn't any space left,' gushed Babu.

'See, we have a lot of things to deal with. You manage it somehow,' replied Raghunath.

'Sir, the people are aware of the fact that K-Kare company took the contract for 60 crore rupees to deal with the issue. If you don't solve the problem, the news will spread out. I'm trying my best to keep things safe. But you have to do something about it,' pleaded Babu.

'Okay, I'll look into it,' Raghunath hung up the call.

Raghunath walked across his room in the party office and closed the door. By pressing a few icons on his phone, he dialled the person he wanted.

'Comrade Ragesh Nakuty, lal salaam!' saluted Raghunath.

'Lal salaam! Tell me, Comrade Raghunath,' said Ragesh.

'Some problems are being reported from Brahmanagar,' said Raghunath. 'We have to clear the garbage. It seems that people are aware of the contract of our company.'

'What happened?' queried Ragesh.

'The space is running out. It's been more than five years since we took the contract to recycle the waste. But we haven't done anything,' said Raghunath.

'What are the options?' asked Ragesh.

'We should've bought the recycling machines with the money we got. We have no equipment at all. Neither do we have any staff except for that idiot operations officer,' stated Raghunath.

'That money went to everyone, Comrade Raghunath. Although K-Kare is my company, the 60 crores were divided among every councillor of our party, the mayor, the chief minister, and of course, you and me. There is nothing left to buy a recycling unit nor outsource the job to another company,' said Ragesh calmly.

'What should we do now?' asked Raghunath, nervously.

'It's just garbage, right? It's not a nuclear reactor. Tell them to burn it,' replied Ragesh.

'Burn it? Will it solve the issue?' asked Raghunath.

'Of course. That's what we do in our homes, right? Just burn some piles, and it'll create some space. There is nothing more to be done about this,' Ragesh then hung up the phone.

Comrade Raghunath sighed. He took the phone to dial but then put it back without proceeding to make the call. He left the party office and started his car to drive to the Brahmanagar landfill.

The stench of Brahmanagar managed to invade the closed windows of Raghunath's car as he approached the landfill. It was still some five kilometres from the destination. Raghunath felt as though the smell burned the hairs in his nostrils. The comrade still drove further until he felt he couldn't drive any nearer. He stopped and called Babu.

'Hey, it's me, Raghunath.'

'Tell me, sir. What should we do about the garbage?' asked Babu frantically.

'I'm sending you the location where I am now. It's nearby. Just come here,' replied Raghunath.

Babu opened the location sent by Raghunath on WhatsApp. He then left his office, mounted his motorcycle, and drove straight to the location. Raghunath was waiting for Babu in his sedan car. The comrade gestured for him to get in, and Babu did so.

'So, what should we do about the rising garbage? Is the recycling machine ready?' asked Babu.

'There is no recycling unit. You just have to resort to the old ways,' said Raghunath.

'What do you mean?' gulped Babu.

'You have to burn it. Not all at once. Do it slowly. Day by day. No one will notice,' muttered Raghunath.

'Sir, what about K-Kare? They were paid to take care of this mess,' said Babu in utmost dissatisfaction.

'How many years do you plan to spend your life here in this hellhole? Don't you want to escape Brahmanagar? Just do as I say, and I will secure a decent job for you anywhere else in Kerala,' stated Raghunath.

'But… what about K-Kare?' asked Babu.

'K-Kare isn't the one who needs promotion or an escape from Brahmanagar. If you handle this on your own, then I can guarantee you a new government job wherever you want,' Raghunath said with confidence.

Babu kept his silence for a while. The images of him working in a glistening air-conditioned office somewhere in the capital city rushed through his mind. It had been years since he dragged his life through the hell called Brahmanagar. When it opened, the government promised that it would possess a garbage recycling unit with cutting-edge technology. The local government of the city banned households from burning garbage. They made it mandatory for every resident of the city to give their garbage, whether recyclable or non-recyclable, to the Municipal Corporation staff who would come every week to collect the waste. This wasn't a free service either. Each house had to pay Rupees One Hundred per month to the Municipal Corporation for this. Even if a house was empty and locked, the owner had to pay for it or face legal charges from the local government. The tons of garbage began piling up in the Brahmanagar landfill. The staff were told that the K-Kare company, which won the contract to recycle the waste, would take care of the mess. Babu was appointed as the manager and he began waiting for the K-Kare company to do its duties. However, the company never came and the garbage began mounting up. The stench of the garbage started haunting the neighbouring areas as well. The value of plots around the area plummeted. Residents left the area without selling their lands as no one would buy them near Brahmanagar. Those who couldn't afford to escape continued living nearby, fraught and endangering their health with polluted substances soaring from the landfill. Babu wanted to escape from his job and this was the perfect opportunity to do so.

'Yes. I'll do the needful,' muttered Babu.

'But you have to do it discreetly,' said Raghunath.

'Sure.'

Babu went back to the landfill. There were still some staff doing their jobs. As the clock struck 5, everyone began leaving all at once. Babu stayed back. He walked through the mountains of garbage. He realized that it wasn't an easy task. He was aware of the seriousness. There are health risks to burning garbage, especially the non-biodegradable ones. That's the sole reason the government banned burning waste in households. Realizing this, Babu formed a small heap of garbage using some iron rods a decent distance away from a giant mount of garbage. He sprayed some kerosene over it and lit it with fire. It started burning with the sharp smell of burnt plastic. Babu knew breathing in burning plastics meant health hazards. Therefore, he stayed away, watching it burn. The plastics crumbled, shrunk, and fried. The heap didn't vanish but changed its form to a small black semi-solid mass. However, there was no fire to be seen. It seemed as though the flame had died out. The whole process took ten minutes and nothing significant happened. Babu realized this wasn't going to be practical and decided he would let Raghunath know that he was out of this operation. Discontented, Babu left for home.

It was a windy night. Babu was sleeping comfortably in his home. Meanwhile, back in Brahmanagar, the wind invigorated some sparks still silently and slowly burning the heap of garbage that Babu had lit. The sparks turned into a fire and it engulfed the heap, burning it mercilessly. That wasn't all. The flames enlarged by the wind and skipped across, lighting a small dry piece of paper lying on the huge mount of garbage. The burning paper spread its heat to the nearby waste and the progression grew exponentially in the darkness.

The next day, on his way to Brahmanagar, Babu felt as though it would rain. The sun was masked by the overcast sky. But as he went nearer, he realized that it wasn't the clouds hiding the sun, it was the smoke. The other staff of the landfill were standing outside. Babu left his motorcycle on the road and rushed. He couldn't enter the landfill premises because of the smoke. The black toxic smoke engulfed the area. On top of that, the fiery flames spread like wildfire. The emitted heat was unbearable. The residents of the neighbourhood gathered outside the colony to witness the doomsday.

Babu called the police and the fire department. However, the press arrived at the scene before the emergency department. Hundreds of cameras accompanied by their corresponding reporters captured the apocalyptic moment and narrated the story to the millions at home. The fire brigade arrived and watched the horror in shock. The firefighters saw the biggest fire in their lives.

The chief of the fire staff called Babu and asked him what happened.

'I don't know. I came in the morning to find this fire. I have no idea how it happened,' cried Babu.

It was no time to find the cause of the fire; it was time to stop it. The fire brigade chief was well aware of his priorities and ordered his ranks to enter the landfill and start the operation. There was a limit to how far the firefighters and their trucks could reach. The fire was dancing as all hell broke loose. The pressurized water from their hoses couldn't reach the fire.

'We need air support! We need air support!' yelled one of the firefighters.

'This isn't America,' said the chief to a co-firefighter, 'It will take days for us to mobilize choppers to drop water here in addition to getting permission for that and getting the funds for it to be allocated. This is Kerala.'

The cops rushed to the neighbouring colony and warned the people to get away as far as possible from the area.

'But we have nowhere to go,' said a lady.

'If you stay here, you will die of poisoning. Go somewhere. To a relative's house or a friend's. Somewhere but not here,' the cop screamed.

The miserable crowd ran with their belongings as someone told them the fire might burn their houses as well. Within a few hours, there weren't any residents in the area. All of them were evacuated with the help of government buses.

Babu watched the scenes unfold in horror. He felt as though he had unleashed a monster. He was sure that hundreds would succumb to health issues or even death as a result of this disaster, and he was responsible for it.

Babu tried calling Raghunath repeatedly, but the calls weren't accepted. Meanwhile, Raghunath was watching the entire event on a news channel on his TV. He was accompanied by other activists in the party office.

'Who is so foolish to have lit the garbage?' grumbled a young comrade.

Raghunath didn't hear it. He was immersed in the terrifying visuals.

The inmates of the party office felt as though it was getting dark. The sunlight was vanishing. They went outside to find the black smoke swamping the shining sun. It became dark.

The people of the city fell into suffocation. They breathed toxic air. All those plastic molecules flew in the air with carbon monoxide smoke. It made its way towards the inner bodies of innocent people, forever damaging their health. It was chaos. The city had succumbed.

# 10

Avinash Mahadevan got off the train at the railway station of his hometown. The fact that he promised Alma he would spend the next few days with his parents annoyed him. Perhaps, it might be the only lie he had told her.

Avinash took a taxi and went straight to a place on the outskirts of the city. He opened the gate to find some little boys playing football. While walking to an old building adjacent to a newly constructed multi-story building, the football rolled over to him. He dribbled the ball away from the boy who tried to take it. However, the luggage he was carrying prevented him from moving any further. He passed the ball to the boy and went to the old building.

A forty-year-old man was arranging some furniture in the main hall. Seeing the guest, the man rushed toward him.

'Avinash, my boy! I can't believe you're here!' chortled the man.

'Kuttetta! You say that as if I don't come here often,' said Avinash.

'Visiting here once in a while doesn't qualify as often,' joked Kuttetta. 'Come in. You must be tired. Where are you coming from?'

'I had an archaeological excavation in Madhya Pradesh. I could've gone straight home, but then I realized that there is no one waiting for me there. So, I thought it's better I stay here for a few days instead. This is where I spent my childhood growing up as an orphan,' said Avinash with a tone of mild seriousness.

'No one is an orphan here. That's why our institution is called Balasadanam, the home for kids, and not an orphanage. Your father, Mahadevan Ji, was a vigorous activist for our organization. Unfortunately, his activism got him killed along with your mother. His contributions to society and the nation are substantial. Maybe the political party he was affiliated with would have forgotten him, but not us,' Kuttetta said emotionally.

Avinash stayed silent for a while.

'You can use my room to freshen up. I'll bring tea for you. I'll call Ramachandran Ji and others about your arrival. They'll come. It's been a long time since we all have seen you,' said Kuttetta.

Avinash thanked him and took his luggage to Kuttetta's room. While taking a shower, he remembered his childhood days spent here. The institution was part of an organization that had a wide variety of social activities all across the nation. Avinash became a history enthusiast after going through the large collection of books on Indian culture and heritage in the Balasadanam library.

Nevertheless, Avinash wasn't feeling comfortable. He had lied to Alma. In reality, he had no idea why he lied. Maybe he feared Alma wouldn't be interested in him if he revealed the truth. Avinash knew he couldn't keep this lie any longer. He remembered the message Alma sent asking him to send her a photo of him with his parents. Avinash thought it would be better to tell her the truth.

After taking a shower, Avinash stood at the entrance of the old building, his eyes tracing the familiar contours of the building where he had spent his childhood. The memories flooded back—of laughter echoing in the corridors, the smell of food wafting through the air, and the caretakers who had become his surrogate family.

It was a working day. There weren't many children there as most of them had gone to school. Avinash spent much of his time checking the garden and going through the photo albums of the institution. Kuttetta took him to the new building of the complex, where there were new dorms and a hall. Amidst all this, Avinash was sending messages to Alma.

'Send a photograph with your parents. I'll only reply after I see one,' she replied.

Avinash couldn't send her any messages after that, and he engaged himself in interacting with the staff of the institution, who updated him about the place's functioning.

Time went by, and the children came back from school.

'Avinashetta!' one of the older boys shouted, rushing towards Avinash.

'It's good to see you, Aswin. How's your studies going?' Avinash asked, his eyes scanning the room for familiar faces.

'I'm more into football, brother. I'm also participating in the State Sports Meet representing my school,' replied Vinod.

'Wow! That's wonderful.'

'Come, let's play after tea,' Aswin took Avinash to the canteen.

Sipping tea alongside piping-hot vadas, Avinash later joined the young lads outdoors, immersing himself in the ritual of their evening exercises. Avinash used to do yoga and play kabbadi here on the same piece of ground for years without a break. It had been a while since he had played games with anyone. He felt rejuvenated and alive. The green surroundings aided in the feeling as well.

Avinash spent the rest of the day engaging with the children, sharing stories of his archaeological adventures and inspiring them with dreams of exploration. His eyes sparkled with passion as he described the ancient artifacts he had discovered, transporting the children to distant lands and times.

After dinner, Avinash proposed a unique activity. He had brought a collection of artefacts, ranging from ancient coins to pottery shards. Not all of them were original. Some were just models. The children gathered around him, their eyes wide with wonder.

'This is a piece of history,' Avinash explained, holding up an intricately carved relic. 'And each of you has the power to uncover stories hidden in the past. Who knows, one day you might become an archaeologist like me!'

'I'm interested in digging up dinosaur bones instead,' said a curly-haired boy.

'He watched Jurassic Park recently. That's why the craze,' laughed another boy.

'If you're sincere in your ambitions and ready to take whatever difficult path to achieve them, then nothing can stop you,' Avinash said, trying to inspire the kid. But he knew this was just a usual dialogue of all motivational speakers.

The children eagerly examined the artefacts, their imaginations running wild. Avinash's heart swelled with joy as he witnessed the curiosity and excitement in their eyes.

While in bed, trying to sleep, Avinash stared at the WhatsApp chat with Alma. She hadn't sent any replies to any of his messages. Not even the usual 'Good Night, dear.' With a heavy heart, Avinash tried to sleep.

Avinash knew about the daily routine of the Balasadanam. The residents were supposed to wake up at 5 am. After getting ready, they had to assemble in the courtyard for the morning prayers. Avinash readily participated in all these activities. He witnessed the children getting ready for school as he was having breakfast.

As Avinash exited the canteen, an unusual darkness cast a shadow over the cheerful scene. Confused whispers spread among the children as they gazed upward, their innocent faces morphing into expressions of concern. Avinash, sensing the sudden shift, looked at the sky for answers.

He stepped outside just in time to witness the transformation of the sky. Once a serene blue, it had turned into a foreboding black. A strange unease settled over the building as Avinash looked up, sharing the bewilderment of the children.

Kuttetta, sensing something amiss, joined Avinash outside. 'What's happening, Avinash?'

Avinash pointed at the sky. 'I have no idea, Kuttetta. It's like the world just turned upside down.'

A sinister odour crept in, invading the nostrils of the children with a pungent and acrid scent. It was a noxious cocktail of burning plastic, chemicals, and the charred remains of discarded waste.

'Let's find out. Gather the children inside,' said Kuttetta, squinting at the darkened sky.

The atmosphere shifted from confusion to urgency as Kuttetta's orders resonated through the Balasadanam. The children, sensing the gravity of the situation, hurried indoors. Avinash and Kuttetta followed.

Inside the common area, the children huddled together, their eyes darting between Avinash and Kuttetta for an explanation. Before anyone could speak, the first cough echoed through the room, followed by another. The air, once crisp, now carried an unfamiliar acrid scent.

Avinash, his brows furrowed, approached one of the older boys, Rahul, who was coughing profusely. 'Are you alright, Rahul?' he asked.

'It's hard to breathe, brother,' replied Rahul, struggling to catch his breath.

The realization struck Avinash, and he exchanged a worried glance with Kuttetta. Without delay, Avinash reached for the remote and turned on the television on the opposite wall of the room. The news channels were ablaze with reports of a fire in Brahmanagar, spewing toxic smoke into the air.

On the TV, Avinash observed the unfolding tragedy. Firefighters battled the raging landfill inferno. Their silhouettes were barely visible through the thick smoke.

'That's why the sky turned black. We need to do something,' said Kuttetta, his face contorted with concern.

Avinash, watching the news intently, felt a lump in his throat.

'The smoke is toxic. We need to get the children out of here,' Avinash yelped.

'Evacuate to the basement. It's safer down there. I'll alert the staff,' said Kuttetta.

As the staff members hurriedly guided the children to the basement, the severity of the situation became increasingly apparent. The acrid air invaded the building and triggered a chorus of coughs and wheezes. Avinash, guiding the children, felt a weight on his chest, a psychological manifestation of the impending danger.

In the basement, Avinash gathered the children, attempting to provide reassurance amid the growing unease.

'We're going to be okay down here. Just stay calm, and we'll get through this together,' Avinash consoled.

As they huddled in the dimly lit space, Avinash noticed the immediate health effects taking a toll on the children. One of the younger boys, Manish, collapsed to the floor, unconscious. Panic rippled through the group.

Avinash, rushing to Manish's side, called for Kuttetta.

'Kuttetta, we need help here!'

Kuttetta, his face etched with concern, knelt beside Avinash and Manish.

'We can't wait any longer. We need to get these kids to a safer place,' said Kuttetta with resolve.

'That's what I was thinking as well,' said Avinash. 'This smoke won't subside until the fire is put out. We have to go as far from the epicentre as possible.'

'Let's take the kids to the Community Health Centre in the next district. The smoke won't reach there,' suggested Kuttetta.

The staff, though visibly shaken, rallied to support the children. Their noses were covered with masks and towels, and they all boarded the institution's bus. The journey through the smoky streets was arduous, each step accompanied by the unsettling sounds of coughing and wheezing.

As the bus rolled into the outskirts of the once serene city, an eerie haze hung heavily in the air. The sun, attempting to break through the thick clouds of toxic smoke, only succeeded in casting a dim, apocalyptic glow upon the desolation below. The bus windows rattled with the muffled sounds of distant chaos. The passengers of the bus exchanged uneasy glances as the severity of the situation became apparent.

The bus needed to pass through the city to exit it. As the bus trundled further, the scene outside grew increasingly nightmarish. The city had transformed into a dystopian landscape, where thick smoke billowed from the smouldering landfill, shrouding buildings in a disturbing veil. Abandoned cars lined the streets, their owners having fled in panic, leaving behind silent witnesses to the unfolding disaster.

Emergency vehicles with flashing lights sped past the bus. Their sirens wailed mournfully in the distance. The police, clad in protective gear, stood at strategic points, desperately trying to maintain order amidst the chaos. Through loudspeakers, their commands echoed through the smoke-laden air, instructing residents to evacuate immediately and seek shelter indoors or leave the city as soon as possible.

Anxious faces peered out from behind boarded-up windows as the bus continued its ominous journey. Some residents, overcome by fear and uncertainty, stumbled along the deserted streets, clutching makeshift masks to their faces in a feeble attempt to shield themselves from the toxic air. Coughs and wheezes echoed through the air, the grim soundtrack of a community under siege.

As the minutes ticked by, the police amplified their instructions over loudspeakers, urging everyone to stay indoors and seal their homes against the toxic fumes. The town stood paralyzed, held captive by an unseen enemy that permeated the very air they breathed.

Inside the bus, a grave silence enveloped the children as they contemplated the uncertainty of their fate. The toxic montage outside continued to unfold. It was a display of a town in the grip of a disaster caused by humans.

The bus, after a prolonged journey finally arrived at the haven of the community centre situated beyond the city confines.

Upon reaching the community centre, medical staff distributed masks and water. The children, still recovering from the toxic exposure, found some relief in the cleaner air. Avinash, Kuttetta, and the staff worked together to organize the children, doing their best to provide comfort amidst the chaos.

As the day wore on, the immediate toxic health effects on the children remained a grave concern. Medical attention became a priority as more children showed signs of respiratory distress. Emergency medical teams arrived, distributing inhalers and oxygen masks to alleviate their suffering.

Avinash, watching the children receive medical care, felt a mix of relief and anguish. The images of their struggling faces lingered in his mind.

Night fell, but the toxic smoke still shrouded the city.

The children, exhausted and scared, lay on beds in the community health centre. Avinash, Kuttetta, and the staff took turns keeping a watchful eye on them.

Avinash found himself engrossed in the distressing narrative unfolding on his smartphone screen. The news videos showed the relentless battle against the Brahmanagar fire.

As Avinash scrolled through the updates, each frame revealed a haunting reality - the inferno that had consumed the landfill defied conventional efforts to be quenched. Firefighters, clad in protective gear that seemed inconsequential against the ferocity of the blaze, fought a valiant yet seemingly futile struggle. The inferno, fuelled by an amalgamation of refuse and hazardous materials, resisted their attempts with an almost wicked willpower.

Avinash winced at the footage depicting the perilous conditions faced by the firefighters. Their silhouettes emerged from the billowing smoke, their movements choreographed in desperate harmony. However, the news anchor's dire tone conveyed the harsh truth – the firefighters, the unsung heroes of this inferno, were not only battling the flames but were themselves succumbing to the consequences of their valour.

Reports trickled in, revealing the toll exacted on these brave souls. Avinash couldn't shake the sense of helplessness that enveloped him as he witnessed their sacrifices unfold on the smartphone in his hand.

Amidst the chaos, the news report showcased an announcement: the District Collector, had issued an uncompromising order. The city was now deemed untenable for habitation. Every resident was mandated to evacuate.

Avinash felt a profound heaviness in his chest. The District Collector's directive was a stark acknowledgment of the magnitude of the crisis – a city, now rendered inhospitable by the unyielding force of nature, had reached the cliff of its endurance.

As Avinash continued to absorb the unfolding calamity through his smartphone screen, a realization settled upon him. Weeks, not mere days, would pass before the insatiable fire could be tamed. The city, in its present state, seemed destined for an extended period of torment. The images of the firefighters' struggles and the resolute evacuation order etched an indelible mark on Avinash's consciousness.

However, he knew something more than that. He knew about K-Kare and its contract with Brahmanagar.

It was as if echoes reverberated across the rooms and halls when the final statement of a man thundered. Every smartphone held by the party workers and every television hung on the wall showed the same thing: the final self-recording video of Babu, the manager of the Brahmanagar landfill. While news channels aired the video under the headline 'Chernobyl of Kerala', those watching on their smartphones had direct links to Babu's video on his Facebook account.

'It is not my fault. The K-Kare company was paid 60 crores by the government to deal with the garbage of Brahmanagar. However, they never did. For years, waste piled up, and as the landfill manager, I tried my best to get K-Kare to deal with it. But I couldn't even reach them. It was Comrade Raghunath who told me to burn the garbage, and I never thought it would spiral into a disaster. I can't watch this disaster unfold, so I decided to end my life with you all as witnesses.'

Babu placed the phone in such a way that it could capture the entire room, revealing a hanging rope on the ceiling fan. As the live video feed broadcasted his activities, Babu climbed the chair and hung himself to death. The live feed continued to air a lifeless body.

Ragesh Nakutty watched the entire scene unfold on the television in his cabin, accompanied by some of his comrades.

'Will this cause any trouble, comrade?' muttered a loyal comrade in Ragesh's ear, bending down.

'Never. Nobody knows about my connection with K-Kare,' replied Ragesh confidently.

Politicians and activists took centre stage, their impassioned voices echoing through the airwaves. Accusations flew like arrows, each one finding its mark on the beleaguered shoulders of the Municipal Corporation. The blame game unfolded before their eyes, a scripted drama of finger-pointing and deflection.

In the midst of the turmoil, investigative journalists sought answers in the shadows. The elusive K-Kare company became a phantom haunting the narrative. The question of its whereabouts lingered. The silence that followed the inquiry left just a void.

The news reports also showed montages of people being admitted to hospitals, visuals of ambulances, and firefighters trying to put out the fire. Flames roared in the backdrop as firefighters battled an inferno that seemed to mirror the societal blaze fuelled by negligence. A scorecard of the death toll stood stoically on the side of the screens.

The atmosphere in Ragesh's living room crackled with anticipation as the television screen transformed with an announcement. The familiar blue and red BREAKING NEWS banner took the attention of Ragesh and his comrades. They pivoted toward the TV.

The news reporter's voice surged with excitement. The screen transitioned to a vivid display of a Facebook post. The voice of the news reporter, a steady guide through the digital landscape, narrated the contents of the post.

Ragesh sweated as the text 'OWNER OF K-KARE FOUND' appeared on the screen. The Facebook post read: 'K-Kare, the company that received 60 crores from the Municipal Corporation to address the waste issue of the Brahmanagar landfill, is owned by none other than Ragesh Nakutty. The paper company was primarily set up to receive such contracts from the leftist government so that the comrades could share the taxpayers' money among themselves. It is unfortunate that the entire city has collapsed, and many people had to die because of this corruption by Ragesh Nakutty.'

All the comrades in the building came to Ragesh's office. The room filled with a diverse mix of voices, each bringing with them a blend of curiosity, concern, and perhaps a tinge of jealousy.

'Comrade, is this true?' asked someone from the group.

'No, it's just an accusation,' said Ragesh, controlling his emotions. 'Even the chief minister's daughter has a company in Bangalore to receive bribes. This is not something like that.'

‘Why are you suddenly bringing the CM into this?’ asked someone.

‘Look, comrades,’ Ragesh’s loyal assistant intervened, ‘This FB post is written by someone who usually accuses Comrade Ragesh. Don’t believe him.’

A fleeting sense of oversight surged through him as he comprehended that he had neglected to inspect the authorship of the pivotal social media post.

The name, when revealed, resonated like a resounding echo in Ragesh's consciousness – Avinash Mahadevan.

Consumed by a turbulent storm of anger and hatred, Ragesh's reaction was visceral. In an explosive surge, he propelled himself from his seat, abandoning the confines of his office in a whirlwind of emotions. He hastily made his way to his car. The engine roared to life as he peeled away from the building, the tires screeching against the pavement

The road stretched out before him as he navigated the streets. There was no toxic smoke, as he was safely 200 kilometres away from Brahmanagar. Ragesh's fingers danced on his phone, dealing a number with swift and purposeful motions.

‘Come to my residence!’ he ordered.

Ragesh arrived at his imposing three-story house. Two muscular men were positioned strategically near the entrance. They entered the house after Ragesh.

‘Find this man,’ said Ragesh after showing the Facebook profile of Avinash Mahadevan on his smartphone.

‘Sure. Do you want us to finish him off?’ asked one of the men.

'No, he is being noticed by everyone now. If something happens to him, I will surely be blamed,' replied Ragesh.

'Then what do you want us to do with him?'

'Hack into his personal stuff. Find something sensitive. Use that to lock him up. Make sure it doesn't trace back to us,' said Ragesh, as though he had rehearsed it.

The two men left the premises as Ragesh scrolled through Avinash's Facebook timeline. He saw multiple posts written by Avinash against him. He was convinced that this so-called environmental activist was targeting him.

Meanwhile, back in Brahmanagar, the authorities, desperately trying to quell the raging flames, were engaged in a battle against both the fire and the systemic corruption that had long saturated their ranks.

The firefighters who were clad in shoddy, low-quality anti-fire uniforms that provided little protection against the merciless blaze breathed the toxic fumes that choked the air. The smoke, born out of non-decaying waste clung to their bodies.

After relentless efforts, permission was finally granted to employ helicopters for the mission. However, there weren't any experienced persons to operate them. Nonetheless, a couple of choppers with large bucket-like structures hanging beneath them took flight over the city.

With a surreal manoeuvre over the lake, they swooped down, scooping massive volumes of water, and ascended to release their liquid payload over the flaming landfill. It was a spectacle that, at first, held promise - a desperate attempt to drown the fire in gallons of water. Yet, it had an impact similar to tossing a mere teaspoon of sugar into the vastness of the ocean.

The unyielding relentless fire roared on defiantly as though mocking the feeble efforts to subdue its fury. The sky stayed gloomy with thick, toxic blackness. Night descended early upon Brahmanagar.

News reporters somehow donned ultra-modern smoke masks that offered a stark contrast to the makeshift protection worn by the authorities. While the journalists adapted to the chaos with cutting-edge technology, the brave men in uniforms clung to towels wrapped haphazardly around their faces.

The broadcasted visuals reached across the nation like a gripping scene from a Hollywood apocalyptic blockbuster. Viewers, far removed from the unfolding calamity, were thrust into a surreal world that felt more like fiction. But they still held onto the belief that such disasters would never affect them.

Avinash, safely distanced from ground zero, was relieved that the children of the Balasadana were receiving treatment at the Community Health Centre. However, he remained concerned about the lasting effects of the disaster. This was when he received a call from someone he hadn't heard from in a couple of days – Alma.

‘I saw you on TV, rescuing some kids from an orphanage,’ said Alma.

‘There weren’t any TV reporters there,’ Avinash wondered aloud.

'It seemed as though someone shot it on a mobile camera,' said Alma. 'What were you doing in that orphanage? Weren't you supposed to be with your family?'

'Well, those orphans are my family,' replied Avinash.

'Finally, you said it,' said Alma. 'Why couldn't you have just told me this earlier? I already knew.'

'Wait, how do you know?' asked Avinash, surprised.

'Boy, we studied in the same school. I know a lot about you. What made you lie to me?' Alma's tone was a mix of dissatisfaction and triumph.

Avinash pondered for a moment. Did he actually lie, or was he just not correcting anyone who assumed he had parents? Even he didn't bother to correct Prof. Ahmed when he talked about Avinash's parents.

'I didn't lie purposefully,' replied Avinash.

'Sometimes you're a mystery, Avinash,' mused Alma.

There was no reply.There were only mild grunts from the other end.

'Avinash! Avinash!' called Alma, but he didn't reply.

Then the phone hung up. What might have happened to him? Did he just cut the call because of anger?

Alma called back and heard that the phone was switched off.

'He must be angry or discontented,' she thought. 'Let him take his time and call back.'

In reality, Avinash was confused and dumbfounded. He was blinded by a black cloth and didn't know who was forcefully taking him. He sensed there were three of them, taking him in some car. The unknown men tied his hands behind his back with a plastic rope and gagged him. Questions crashed into his mind, but he could only wonder about them.

Although his mouth was blocked, he could still smell. Gradually, as the car moved, Avinash started to sense the smell of toxic smoke.

'They're taking me back to the city. But why?'

As minutes passed, the stench of toxic smoke penetrated his nose like blades.

The car came to a halt. The abrupt stop jolted Avinash from his uneasy reverie. In blindness, he sensed rather than saw the presence of the men trying to overpower him. Hands seized him, their grip firm as they pushed, pulled, and dragged him toward an uncertain destination.

Amidst the chaos of his disorientation, there were steps. Blindly, he was coerced to ascend, his feet were guided by the relentless pressure of the men surrounding him.

Avinash found himself anchored by the firm grasp of his captors.

He was pushed to the floor. His hands somehow freed themselves from the loosely tied plastic ropes. He immediately pulled off the black cloth covering his face and took out the gag. He found himself inside a room with deteriorating walls. He realized it was the Ghost Apartment near Brahmanagar, abandoned three decades ago. The only exit from the room was locked, and he could hear the men outside as they walked away. Avinash rushed to the door.

'At least tell me why you're doing this to me!' bellowed Avinash.

'Don't you dare try to take away a girl from our community!' yelled back someone in a Malabari slang.

The only other way outside was through the windows with no bars. However, the room was filled with black smoke, and he could virtually see nothing. He was sure he was on some top floor, as he remembered walking up the steps. It was obviously dangerous to attempt an escape through the window with zero visibility.

Each inhale was a searing plunge into a world of acrid torment. It assaulted his senses with a ferocity that threatened to overwhelm him. It clawed its way into his lungs, leaving a bitter residue that burned with the intensity of a thousand infernos.

In the foggy room, his eyes stung and watered against the assault of the noxious fumes. Every breath was a battle. The air itself seemed to pulse with ghostly energy. His heart thundered in his chest. With every beat, he could feel the weight of time pressing down upon him, forcing him forward even as the smoke threatened to choke the life from his body.

He coughed violently, each spasm wracking his body with jerky force. The acrid taste of smoke filled his mouth, choking off his breath in a cruel vice grip. With eyes squeezed shut against the torment, he sought refuge in the darkness behind his lids.

In that moment of searing pain and suffocating despair, he realized this was the end. The culmination of all his struggles, hopes, and dreams reduced to nothing but ashes in the merciless inferno.

Minutes passed like an eternity suspended in time. Slowly, agonizingly, the room began to emerge from the suffocating shroud of smoke. With each passing moment, clarity pierced through the haze, dispelling the choking fog that had engulfed everything in its path. The air gradually transformed into a pristine expanse of clarity and purity.

With trembling limbs and a heart heavy with dread, Avinash slowly walked towards the window. He expected to see the Brahmanagar landfill's fire being put out by the firefighters.

But what he saw beyond the confines of his refuge left him reeling in disbelief.

Brahmanagar had been wiped clean from the face of the Earth. Where once stood the sprawling expanse of the landfill now lay only a vast wilderness, overrun by a riotous explosion of grassy life.

It was as if the very earth itself had risen up in rebellion, reclaiming its territory. Thick vines snaked their way across the landscape, their sinuous tendrils weaving greenery that stretched as far as the eye could see. Roots delved deep into the soil, anchoring the land in a primal embrace that defied the ravages of fire and destruction. It was the first time in his life he witnessed leaf, vines, and roots overpowering fire.

# 12

The daylight was coming to a close when Suresh Tiwari found himself ensconced in the comfort of his government quarters. His gaze was fixated upon the flickering screen of his television set. The live telecast of reports and murmurs unfolded news both perplexing and miraculous: the Brahmanagar landfill, a monstrous inferno, had vanished into the ether, consumed by an entanglement of vines and resolute roots. Yet, Suresh's reaction was not one of astonishment, but rather a shiver of fear coursing through his spine.

For Suresh, this was not the first encounter with such uncanny phenomena. He had witnessed with his own eyes the iron sinews of a railway track yield to the insistent embrace of nature's whims, vanishing like spectres into the abyss. And before that, the haunting scene of a colossal factory pipe being ensnared in an intricate knot by the same forces.

A profound unrest gripped Suresh's soul. Was this

phenomenon confined to the confines of his nation, or did its reach extend far beyond the borders of familiarity? He grappled with the balance between fear and wonder, unsure whether to embrace the growing tide of nature's resurgence with joy or cower in the shadow of impending apocalypse.

Suresh Tiwari's walls bore no family photos. Instead of cherished photographs capturing moments of love and laughter the walls had an array of mementos, tokens bestowed upon him by various organizations.

Amidst this sparse interior, an oasis of greenery flourished in the form of indoor plants nestled within small pots and bottles. On the balcony, larger pots hosted a vibrant miniature landscape of foliage.

Suddenly, the TV screen went blank with a 'No Input' message. With a furrowed brow, Suresh tried changing channels and restarting the TV, but nothing helped. He attempted to access the news on his smartphone. However, there was neither internet connection nor phone connectivity.

An eerie silence enveloped Suresh. Even the ceiling fan had stopped. Gone were the familiar hums and whirs of modernity, replaced instead by a profound absence of electrical noise—the ceaseless drone of machinery, the cacophony of televisions, the rhythmic thrum of refrigerators—all silenced. Only the sound of natural wind remained.

Looking around, Suresh noticed the miniature plants in the bottles and small pots had grown significantly. Where once tender shoots sprouted, now flourished vines, their growth unchecked and unbidden, as if imbued with a voracious hunger for the vessels themselves.

With a sense of gnawing unease, Suresh rose from the couch and left the apartment. He could hear the complaints and confusion of neighbours discussing the sudden stoppage of electricity, internet, and cable connections.

Amidst all this chaos, Suresh found himself lifted by an unexpected sense of liberation. In the absence of explanations and justifications, he discovered a newfound clarity. With a wry smile playing upon his lips, he turned his back on the clamour of civilization and left the neighbourhood, barefoot.

Meanwhile, in another part of the country, a crowd had gathered outside the party office, all awaiting Ragesh Nakutty's statement.

'Comrade, you can't just stay holed up in here,' said a loyal comrade. 'The press is waiting. They want to hear from you.'

'I am not hiding,' retorted Ragesh. 'I'll just tell them I'm not responsible for the landfill fire. Why's everyone so worried? The fire's put out, isn't it?'

'It wasn't put out,' interjected another comrade. 'They're saying some mysterious natural phenomenon swallowed the entire burning landfill, consuming it.'

'We'll save the science fiction for later. I'm going to meet the press,' declared Ragesh resolutely, striding purposefully towards the courtyard.

Emboldened by the fortitude honed through years of artful

deception, Comrade Ragesh Nakutty strode purposefully towards the journalists awaiting him. As he emerged, the cameras and microphones adorned with various news outlets' emblems converged upon him. Ragesh did not falter; he stood resolute.

'Comrade Ragesh, Mr. Nakutty, Sri Ragesh, Ragesh…' each reporter addressed him according to their own perspective. The questions bombarded him like relentless cannon fire besieging a fortress. Ragesh had only one answer: 'I have no connection with K-Kare. These are baseless allegations by the opposition.'

Countless questions continued to barrage the comrade. However, in a matter of fleeting moments, a hush fell over the gathering of journalists and cameramen. They realized their connections to their respective headquarters had been abruptly severed. OB vans stood dormant, network backpacks lay silent, and online-operated cameras ceased their transmissions. Frantic attempts to establish contact with their online operators and bureau chiefs proved useless as dead phone lines blocked their efforts. Realizing this confusion among the reporters, Comrade Ragesh silently retreated to his office.

Meanwhile, chaos vibrated in JiTel Network's regional office. Engineers and other staff members ran around in total confusion. Unlike usual scenarios, there weren't any phone calls disturbing them as all phone connection, from landline to satellite, was cut off.

JiTel's engineers mobilized swiftly, driving their company vehicles to traverse the extensive city. They weren't alone.

Across town, representatives from other network operators prowled the streets, attempting to uncover what was happening.

An unease ambience settled over the streets as dusk descended upon the city, casting a shadow of organic horror upon the unsuspecting citizens. The telecommunication engineers found themselves standing on the cliff of a nightmare. Before them lay a scene straight from the darkest recesses of a twisted imagination. Every antenna, every mobile tower, every satellite dish stood ensnared in a sinister embrace of thick, gnarled vines. Born from the bowels of the earth, these vines of darkness emerged with spiteful intent, entwining themselves around electric wires, cables, posts, and poles alike.

Tarred roads and paved sidewalks buckled and cracked beneath the weight of invasive vegetation. Concrete and metal crumbled before the relentless onslaught of nature's fury. What sent shivers down the spines of all who beheld this unholy spectacle was not the sheer destruction wrought upon the city, but the eerie swiftness with which it had occurred. The proud electrical and digital monuments to human ingenuity now lay twisted, broken husks, consumed by the insatiable hunger of nature itself.

No one knew when this had happened. Usually, it would take decades for nature to reclaim manmade structures. In this case, however, everything occurred without anyone's knowledge, within seconds. Citizens were certain of one thing: there was no hope of regaining network communications or electricity without destroying these vines.

Night hung heavy over the airport, its sprawling runways and towering control tower illuminated by the flickering glow of runway lights.

In the control tower, the air crackled with tension as Air Traffic Control officers watched in horror as their screens blinked to darkness. All at once, the familiar hum of communication with airplanes preparing to land fell silent, leaving pilots and crew members stranded in perilous limbo high above the earth. Panic gripped the control tower as officers grappled with the seriousness of the situation. Without communication with airplanes on the runway, pilots frantically searched for guidance in the darkness.

'It's some kind of temporary network problem!' exclaimed the pilot of Flight 7E 826, his voice tinged with desperation as he tried in vain to establish contact with the control tower, awaiting clearance to take off from the runway.

But as minutes ticked by and the situation grew increasingly dire, ATC officers knew they had no time to spare. With trembling hands and racing hearts, the chief operator issued frantic orders, his voice echoing through the tower.

'Go..Go..Go…send manual messages to all airplanes to return to the tarmacs!' he bellowed, a desperate plea.

Without hesitation, airport staff members rushed to their jeeps, armed with large cards to signal stranded pilots to return to safety. However, as they raced against time to clear the runway, three airplanes remained suspended in the sky, their fate hanging in the balance as they circled above, devoid of guidance from the ground below.

In the cockpit of one such airplane, the AY 9664, the pilot and first officer exchanged worried glances. With fuel levels dwindling and no end to the communication blackout in sight, they knew they had no choice but to circle the skies until order could be restored.

But as minutes stretched into an agonizing eternity, their hopes of swift resolution began to fade. With each passing moment, they realized their fuel was running out, leaving them no option but to land in the darkness below.

Meanwhile, on the runway below, Flight 7E 826 remained stranded in the queue, while another, AY 9664, descended with perilous speed. Oblivious to the impending danger, passengers sat in blissful ignorance.

With a deafening roar, AY 9664 touched down on the runway, its pilots applying brakes with all their might as they fought to bring the aircraft to a halt. But as the plane hurtled towards them, passengers of 7E 826 watched in horror as the approaching aircraft sped towards them. They closed their eyes tight in a moment of sheer terror, willing the nightmare to end. When they opened them again, they found themselves safely on solid ground, mere inches away from disaster. As the airport manager issued an emergency notice suspending all operations until communication could be restored, the airport operated in darkness. Passengers and staff tried to understand what had happened. Those outside witnessed electric wires, communication antennas, and towers decimated by thick vines emerging from the earth.

# 13

The roads were a feverish maze of metal and motion with a chaotic concert of honking horns and screeching tires. Cars and buses careened in every direction with the drivers frantic and their passengers anxious. In this digital blackout, communication was reduced to its most primitive form: face-to-face interaction.

Unable to rely on phones or computers, people were forced to meet in person, passing messages like runners in a relay race. But it wasn't just the common folk feeling the sting of disconnect. The chambers of authority were equally paralyzed. Government officials found themselves blinded by a fog of uncertainty.

As the crisis deepened, everyone felt the economy beginning to crumble. Digital money became useless. Those with cash hoarded it like treasure, while banks stood silent and empty without electricity and computers, their ATMs as lifeless as tombstones. Without electricity, even the most basic services ground to a halt, plunging the world into darkness.

In government offices, leaders sat in limbo, waiting for orders that seemed destined never to arrive. The regional authorities looked to the state government, while the state government strained its eyes toward the central government in New Delhi. But how would they get the instructions? They wondered. All forms of fast communications were unavailable. They had to wait for someone to come all the way from New Delhi. The state government authorities were aware that air and rail services were suspended at the moment, so no one would be arriving immediately.

'It's time to take matters into our own hands,' the Chief Minister of Kerala declared in his chamber in the presence of his cabinet and secretaries. 'There's no point in waiting for instructions from the Centre. This is a national emergency. Maybe we're the only ones suffering from this.'

'No, sir. People have reported similar incidents from our neighbouring states as well,' replied the Chief Secretary.

'We cannot afford to waste another moment,' the Chief Minister bellowed. 'Our local authorities, corporations, panchayats, and municipalities are waiting for our instructions. We have to make a decision now and send officials to all corners of our state to implement our orders.'

'Sir, what do you propose we do?' asked the Chief Secretary.

'Do I look like a disaster management expert to you?' yelled the Chief Minister. 'Where is the minister concerned? Isn't he here?'

Everyone stayed silent and stared at the Chief Minister.

'Don't just sit there clueless. Tell me which ministry handles disaster management and where the responsible minister is?' the Chief Minister repeated.

'Sir,' the Chief Secretary said in a subdued voice, 'it's you. You're in charge of the Home Affairs Ministry.'

'I thought Home Affairs Ministry meant control over the State Police?' the Chief Minister gulped.

'Not just the State Police, sir. The Home Affairs Minister is also responsible for disaster management,' the Chief Secretary added. 'Furthermore, our state also has a statutory non-autonomous body called the Kerala State Disaster Management Authority, which operates under the Chairmanship of the Chief Minister of Kerala.'

'Where is the secretary of this department?' asked the Chief Minister politely.

'Sir, we don't know where he is. I received information that he wasn't present in the office when our staff tried to notify him about this meeting. He may be stuck somewhere else or on the road. We can't locate him. As of now, he is unaware of this meeting. There is no authorized person from the Disaster Management Authority present here at the moment.'

'What should we do now?' asked the Chief Minister.

'Dear Comrade, you have to make the decision, and we will all follow,' stated the Minister of Tourism and Public Works, who also happened to be the Chief Minister's son-in-law.

The Chief Minister, a man in his late 70s, looked at all his ministers, secretaries, and officers in the chamber. All of them seemed helpless and were waiting for his orders. Their faces bore the weight of the crisis, their eyes reflecting a mix of apprehension and hope. A flood of memories washed over the Chief Minister, transporting him back to his youth when he walked defiantly beneath raised swords. His actions during his college days used to instil fear in the hearts of his adversaries. Not even the corruption scandals or political murder allegations against him were able to bring him down. He realized that this was his moment to shine again.

'I have an idea,' said the Chief Minister, as all others in the room extended their eyes and ears toward him. 'Let's cut the vines.'

'What a brilliant idea! Well done, Comrade,' clapped the Minister of Tourism and Public Works.

'We obviously need to do that. I mean, we need a course of action,' pleaded the Chief Secretary.

'A course of action? Hmmm....' the Chief Minister scanned the entire room again. 'Tell everyone to cut the vines. Clear the electric posts and wires first. That should be the priority. Instruct all civilians to participate in the process. Our efforts during the pandemic should serve as inspiration.'

'Alright, I will relay this information. Anything else, sir?' asked the Chief Secretary.

'No...' the Chief Minister stood up to leave, then sat back down. 'Also, spread advertisements and government messages asking people to donate to the Chief Minister's Disaster Relief Fund.'

'Our comrades have already begun asking for donations

with the red bucket,' bragged the Party State Secretary, who was also present at the meeting.

'Good,' cheered the Chief Minister, and he left the chamber.

Meanwhile, the heads of private communication companies didn't wait for orders from the government. They had already sent their employees to cut off the vines and clear their cables, towers, and satellite dishes. As their service engineers were not enough, they also mobilized their office employees and kitchen staff to assist. The task seemed endless. They realized that they needed at least a week to clear their structures from the vines and repair the damages.

By this time, civilians had realized something else. The vines were not only entwining towers and posts but had also started to ensnare bridges. Significant cracks had begun to appear on the bridges. It was only a matter of time before the bridges, succumbing to the weight of their burden and the onslaught of the vines, collapsed into the churning waters below. This would further isolate and cut off major population areas from one another. Civilians braced for impending chaos, knowing that such a scenario would prevent the transportation of emergency supplies.

Alma Fatima watched the employees of JiTel cutting the vines that were ensnaring their satellite tower. Her only entertainment at the moment was watching the scenes unfold from the window of her room. She could hear her parents and brothers through the locked door.

'Attention! Attention! Attention!' Alma heard a passing jeep on the road with a large speaker announcing something. She could also slightly hear the diesel generator powering the microphone and speaker of the jeep. 'In light of the current emergency situation, the Government of Kerala hereby issues a directive to all able-bodied individuals to participate in the reclamation efforts. It is imperative that each and every one of you lends your support to government personnel engaged in clearing vines from electric posts, wires, and other critical structures. We urge you to cooperate fully with authorized personnel and adhere strictly to their instructions. The swift removal of these vines, coupled with the restoration of snapped cables and wires, is essential for the prompt resumption of electricity and communication services. Your assistance in this endeavour is crucial to the well-being and safety of our communities. Together, let us work diligently to overcome this challenge and restore normalcy to our beloved state. Attention! Attention! Attention!'

These announcements, along with sirens from ambulances and fire trucks, were also heard by someone else in another part of the city. Avinash Mahadevan was still trapped in the locked room of the Ghost Apartment. He had been left there to die, breathing the toxic smoke from the nearby Brahmanagar landfill. As chaos raged outside, Avinash remained confined, his fate sealed by forces beyond his control. With each passing moment, the air cleared, yet the cloud of death loomed over him, this time in the form of hunger and despair.

Avinash Mahadevan spent most of his time in the room gazing out of the large, unbarred window. However, realizing there were no escape routes, no pathways, nor stairs, he knew that jumping would lead to certain death. Having accidentally dropped his phone when abducted, he found it impossible to alert anyone to his plight. He was even barefoot at the moment. With his hopes dashed and his spirit broken, Avinash lay in the farthest corner of the room.

As Avinash stood in the silence of the Ghost Apartment, a hush fell over the cityscape. The absence of the usual discord of electrical hums and man-made clamour left an eerie tranquillity in its wake. With a sense of both nervousness and curiosity, Avinash found himself drawn once more to the large window. As he approached, his eyes widened in disbelief at the sight. The Ghost Apartment was now shrouded in a grassy cloak of nature's embrace.

Thick vines, like sinewy serpents, had wound their way around the building. Avinash's heart raced as he took in the sight. For a moment, he remembered the old fairy tale Jack and the Beanstalk. Could it be that these vines, like the fabled beanstalk, held the key to his escape?

With cautious optimism, Avinash tried to climb out of the window, his eyes fixed on the thick, sturdy vine that snaked its way up adjacent to the building. He knew the risks involved—organic materials could be unpredictable, and these vines were no exception. They could be slippery. But in the absence of any other option, he resolved to seize this slender lifeline.

Despite his suspicion that the vines might be slippery, Avinash found solace in the support offered by the lush foliage. Memories of his carefree childhood flooded his mind, transporting him back to simpler times spent swinging from the vines of the banyan tree in Balasadanam.

Taking a deep breath to steady his nerves, Avinash reached

out, his fingers brushing against the smooth surface of the vine. It felt cool and slippery beneath his touch, yet there was an undeniable strength to it. With a silent prayer on his lips, he wrapped his hands around the thick vine and began his descent.

With each step downwards, he treaded carefully, mindful of the slimy surface beneath his feet. As he lowered himself over the edge of the window, the ground far below seemed to stretch out endlessly before him. The wind whispered through the leaves, carrying with it a sense of exhilaration that propelled him onward. With each passing moment, Avinash felt the rush of adrenaline course through his veins, driving him onward despite the natural dangers that lurked below.

With each careful step, Avinash navigated the treacherous terrain of the vine, his heart pounding with every twist and turn. The leaves and twines of the vine provided him with some measure of support, but he knew that one wrong move could send him hurtling to the ground below.

As he descended further, the ground seemed to draw closer with each passing moment, beckoning him with its siren call. Sweat beaded on his brow as he fought to maintain his grip, his muscles straining with the effort. However, despite the physical exertion, there was a sense of exhilaration that overwhelmed him.

But just as Avinash began to feel a glimmer of hope, he heard a sudden crack below. He realized that the vine beneath him had given way, sending him tumbling through the air with a gut-wrenching lurch. For a brief moment, time seemed to stand still as Avinash plummeted towards the ground below, his heart pounding.

But in the nick of time, Avinash's reflexes kicked in, and with a desperate lunge, he managed to grab hold of a nearby branch, arresting his fall with a bone-jarring thud. Pain shot through his body as he struggled to maintain his grip, his fingers slipping on the slick surface of the vine.

With every ounce of strength he possessed, Avinash pulled himself up, his muscles screaming in protest as he fought against the pull of gravity. Inch by agonizing inch, he clawed his way back to safety, his heart continuing to pound with a renewed sense of determination.

And then, with one final burst of effort, Avinash hoisted himself over the edge of the vine and onto solid ground, his chest heaving with exertion as he collapsed in a heap on the grass below. As he lay there panting and exhausted, he looked up at the sky above.

As Avinash lay panting on the grassy ground, his body still trembling from the harrowing descent, his mind raced with a singular purpose: to find his beloved Alma Fatima.

With each passing moment, his heart beat faster, a drumbeat that urged him onward in his quest to find her. She could be in danger, he feared, and he had to find her. She had once told him where she lived. It was in the outskirts of the city. Avinash rose to his feet. He had no phone, watch, or even a pair of footwear. But that didn’t stop him from his quest.

'I think we should help them,' Alma's father, Nazeer said to her brothers, Ajmal and Afsal.

'Yeah, we should. The sooner the electric posts are cleared, the better,' Ajmal replied.

Alma could hear their conversation from inside.

'Shouldn't we unlock her door?' asked Alma's mother.

'Let her be there for a while. We'll be back,' Afsal replied to her mother.

Ajmal and Afsal stepped outside into a scene straight out of a nightmare. The once-familiar streets of their neighbourhood were now engulfed in a tangled web of vines, twisting and writhing like living creatures hungry for prey. It wasn't just the electric and telecommunication poles that bore the burden of nature's onslaught; even the sturdy housing structures and other buildings were being slowly consumed by vines.

Workers from the Kerala State Electricity Corporation and other telecommunication companies toiled tirelessly, fighting to clear the way for progress with each swing of the machete.

As Ajmal and Afsal approached, they couldn't help but marvel at the sheer scale of the devastation before them. Thin vines snaked their way around every corner, their insidious tendrils reaching out like greedy fingers in search of their next victim. However, it was the sight of broken wires and cables strewn haphazardly that caught their attention.

'I still don't understand how these vines were able to snap off the wires,' Ajmal mused, as he turned to one of the KSEC engineers for answers.

The engineer paused, wiping the sweat from his brow with a weary sigh. 'Vines and roots are powerful enough to drill through concrete,' he explained, 'but for them to grow through these structures in just minutes, it's unprecedented.'

As the reality of their situation sank in, Ajmal and Afsal exchanged troubled glances. The neighbourhood had become a battleground. Armed with nothing but choppers and cutters from their humble homes, Ajmal and Afsal, along with other residents, waged a desperate war against the onslaught of vines that threatened to engulf their homes and livelihoods.

The air was filled with the sound of desperate struggle with each swing of the blade and every cut of the vine. The metallic clang of steel against sinewy greenery echoed through the evening. Yet, despite their valiant efforts, the vines continued to advance. With each path cleared, a hundred more appeared, entangling and destroying everything in their path.

It was a never-ending cycle of frustration and despair for the electricians tasked with reconnecting the broken wires. With each repaired connection, another would snap under the weight of the vines' assault, leaving them to start the process anew.

'It's getting dark. We can't continue like this through the night,' Ajmal remarked.

'There are vines too thick for the blades,' the engineer explained, his voice shaded with frustration. 'We need a chainsaw.'

'I can get one from the nearest power tools shop,' Ajmal offered.

'Please bring as much as possible,' the engineer replied.

Ajmal nodded. He made his way to the car porch, his footsteps heavy with apprehension. But what he saw there turned his blood to ice.

Multitudes of vines writhed and twisted underneath the cars, their sinewy tendrils snaking their way around the wheels and undercarriages. The exhausts were blocked, the engines crushed. The cars lay before him as twisted wrecks of metal and glass. The vines had done their work well with their tendrils wrapping around critical pieces. Wires hung limply from their sockets, severed and frayed.

'We'll need someone else's car,' Ajmal announced, still unable to comprehend the fact that his car had been destroyed by mere vines.

However, the situation was the same throughout the neighbourhood. Every car had become immobile.

'What do we do now?' the engineer fretted.

'Don't worry,' Ajmal reassured. 'It's nearby. I'll run over there and bring a chainsaw. Please wait.'

The engineer nodded. 'We have to clear at least some of it before dark,' he replied.

'Don't worry,' Ajmal said while walking away.

The setting sun cast long shadows across the desolate streets as Ajmal set out on his mission. The air was thick with the oppressive scent of decay.

As he made his way through the labyrinthine alleys, Ajmal found himself beset on all sides by the advance of the vines. He stumbled and faltered with each step.

Along the way, he passed countless scenes of chaos and devastation. People from all walks of life had taken up arms against the encroaching vines. But despite their valiant efforts, the vines seemed to multiply with each passing moment with their tendrils creeping ever closer to the heart of the neighbourhood. With time running out and the sun sinking lower in the sky, Ajmal knew he needed to act fast.

Finally, after what felt like an eternity, Ajmal arrived at the power tools shop. The shopkeeper, a weary-looking man with haunted eyes, greeted him with a tired smile.

'You're lucky,' the shopkeeper said, his voice tinged with exhaustion. 'There's only one chainsaw left, and everyone else has already taken the rest.'

The shopkeeper handed Ajmal the chainsaw without taking any money, just wanting it back after use.

With the chainsaw in hand, Ajmal made his way back to the neighbourhood as fast as his legs could carry him. But as he rounded the final corner and beheld the devastation that lay before him, his heart sank like a stone. The sun had already dipped, casting the neighbourhood into darkness that seemed to swallow him whole.

The streets were shrouded in inky blackness, swallowing everything in its path. However, the people of the neighbourhood gathered together, their faces illuminated by the faint glow of flashlights, mobile phone lights with whatever little battery that was left, and flickering torches fashioned from natural fire. Their eyes were haunted, their expressions drawn and weary from days of struggle against the encroaching vines.

They set to work alongside the KSEC workers and other volunteers. The makeshift torches casted eerie shadows against the tangled mass of vines that threatened to engulf their homes and livelihoods. As they laboured tirelessly, the sounds of their efforts echoed through the darkness like a desperate cry. The sharp clang of metal against wood, the low rumble of chainsaws roaring to life, and the crackling hiss of flames as they consumed the tangled mass of vines that ensnared the vital wires, poles, and posts.

But with each step forward, they encountered new horrors that tested their resolve to the breaking point. Thick, sinewy tendrils writhed and twisted in the flickering light, reaching out with a malicious hunger that seemed to defy all reason.

Some claimed to hear whispers in the darkness, a ghostly chorus of voices that whispered of unspeakable horrors lurking just beyond the edge of perception.

And then, just when they thought they could go on no longer, they encountered something that chilled them to the bone. With each swing of the blade, the thick, sinewy tendrils of the vines were rent asunder, their twisted forms falling to the ground in a tangled heap. The KSEC worker moved with a sense of purpose as his movements fluid and precise. He cut through the tangled mass with almost surgical precision. Some civilians stood by his side, their torches providing support and guidance. Together, they cleared an electric post from the suffocating grip of the vines. With the post cleared, he turned to his colleagues, his voice ringing out in the darkness.

'Clamber up,' he urged, gesturing toward the wires that stretched ominously overhead. 'We need to secure those wires before it's too late.'

Without wasting much time, his colleagues ascended the post, their hands shaking with fear as they reached out to grasp the wires that crackled with deadly energy.

Meanwhile, the KSEC worker moved on to another post. This post was different, its thick stems entwined with a strength and tenacity. His grip tightened on the chainsaw.

With a sense of foreboding, he raised the chainsaw high, its blade gleaming in the dim light as he prepared to strike, the roar of the motor echoing through the neighbourhood. But as he moved to make the first cut, a frigid sensation gripped him, a primal instinct warning him of a danger.

With a sudden rustling of foliage, the vines surged forward, their tentacles writhing and twisting. The KSEC worker stumbled back, his heart pounding as he fought to regain his footing.

With a sickening lurch, the vines ensnare him. In an instant, they wrapped themselves around his legs, their grip tightening with unflagging fervency. With a cry of horror, the KSEC worker stumbled backward, his arms flailing wildly as he fought to free himself from the suffocating embrace of the vines. With each passing moment, they tightened their grip, their twisted forms winding their way up his torso with a sickening inevitability.

The KSEC worker screamed in agony as the vines entwined themselves around his arms, locking him in a twisted embrace that left him bound and helpless. His cries echoed through the darkness as everyone in the neighbourhood watched the horrific sight helplessly.

The residents stood frozen in place. Some remained silent, their mouths agape in shock, while others screamed in terror, their voices echoing through the night like a chorus of the damned. But just when they thought the nightmare was over, a new horror emerged from the shadows. From the thick foliage below and the walls covered with writhing vines, new coils snaked forth.

With a sudden lurch, the vines entangled those who held phones or flashlights. Sinewy tendrils wrapped around their arms with unabated intensity and made them helpless to resist. The vines tightened their grip, causing unfortunate victims to scream in agony as their bones snapped and fractured beneath the crushing weight of the persistent assault.

The cries of pain echoed, reverberating off the walls and filling the air with a discord of anguish. But the horror was not confined to their immediate surroundings. From neighbouring areas and far-off corners of the city, the sound of screams and cries echoed through the night.

In the blink of an eye, darkness descended upon the neighbourhood like a suffocating shroud as all flashlights and phones were destroyed. Only those who held natural torches were not attacked.

Ajmal stood frozen in horror as he watched the chaos unfold before him. In the distance, he could hear the panicked screams of his neighbours as they grappled with the sinister forces that now held them. Ajmal's thoughts turned to his brother, Afsal, who stood nearby, oblivious to the danger that lurked just beneath his feet. With a sinking feeling in the pit of his stomach, Ajmal watched as a few sinewy vines slithered across the ground like ravenous serpents.

'Afsal! Run!' Ajmal cried out, his voice choked with fear and desperation. But his warning came too late. A few tendrils of vines slithered onto Afsal and entered through the holes in his pants.

Ajmal seized a machete lying abandoned on the ground and charged toward his brother, his hands trembling with adrenaline as he fought to free him from the clutches of the encroaching vines. With each swing of the blade, he hacked away at the tangled mass. Afsal cried out in pain and horror as the vines tightened their grip by burrowing deep into his flesh.

With a final, desperate effort, Ajmal severed the last of the vines that held his brother captive, his hands slick with sweat and blood as he pulled him free from the suffocating embrace. But there were still lifeless parts of the vines left inside Afsal's thighs. Ajmal took the phone from Afsal's pocket and threw it away. They both ran back to their home.

Alma's heart hammered as she listened to the unsettling cries and screams emanating from the darkness beyond her locked door3. Panic clawed at her throat, threatening to suffocate her as she pounded on the wooden barrier.

'Umma! Bappa! Open the door! Please!' Alma's voice trembled with fear.

In the cruel darkness, she strained her ears, hoping for some sign of rescue. She heard the unmistakable sound of her brothers entering the house.

'Open Alma's door. Let her out,' Ajmal's voice pierced through the darkness.

'What happened? Where are the cries coming from?' Nazeer inquired with concern as her mother, Fatima, fumbled with the lock.

As the door creaked open, she saw the room bathed in the

eerie glow of candlelight. Ajmal and Afsal stood before her with faces contorted in terror. Their chests heaved with frantic breaths, their eyes wide with a terror Alma could not comprehend. Alma realized that whatever horror awaited them beyond that room was far worse than anything she could have imagined.

Alma's brothers recounted the chilling events that had unfolded outside. Each word dripped with dread, painting a picture of terror that gripped the entire family in its icy grasp. They listened to the unimaginable horrors that had unfolded just beyond the safety of their home. The darkness seemed to press in closer, casting sinister shadows. With every detail that spilled from her brothers' lips, Alma's family felt the tendrils of fear wrap around their hearts. They were paralyzed by the sheer magnitude of the horror that had invaded their lives. Their minds raced with frantic thoughts, desperately searching for a way to make sense of the senseless. But as they huddled together in the flickering candlelight, their faces pale with fear, they knew that they were utterly powerless against the wicked forces that lurked just beyond their doorstep.

'What should we do now?' asked Fatima.

'We just have to stay inside the house,' replied Afsal.

'And we have to make sure we don't use any electronic devices,' added Ajmal.

As the family heard the story, they didn't need any further explanation from Ajmal.

With trembling hands and hearts heavy with dread, Alma's

family hastily bolted shut every window and door of their home. The eerie glow of flickering candlelight added to the oppressive atmosphere that hung heavy in the air. Stillness enveloped like a choking veil, broken only by the hushed whispers and ragged breaths of Alma and her family. Each creak of the old house seemed to reverberate through the silence.

However, the night was torn apart by the anguished cries and screams that echoed from across the desolate neighbourhood.

The realization sent a chill down Alma's spine, and she felt her pulse quicken with fear. As the screams grew louder, Alma's family huddled closer together, their eyes wide with terror as they listened helplessly to the sounds of agony that echoed through the night. Each cry was accompanied by a feeling of cold tremor. In the dim light of the candle, their faces were pale and drawn.

While some people were trapped and suffocated inside their homes, others were out on the streets, exposed to all the unknown dangers. A weight of bewilderment pressed down upon Avinash as he navigated the desolate streets barefoot. The shadows seemed to reach out with grasping fingers that threatened to drag him into the abyss. The moon hung heavy in the sky, the only source of illumination with its feeble light. There were no comforting streetlights to guide his way, no reassuring glow of headlights from passing vehicles.

As Avinash made his way toward Alma's house, his senses were assaulted by the sounds of chaos that echoed through the night. The anguished cries of the injured mingled with the desperate pleas of those who were trapped. But he wasn’t alone outside. There were others who were clueless on the road. They were all walking to some destination, while those who were injured were crying in pain on the roadside. Avinash rushed to one of them.

‘What happened?’ he asked, his voice trembling with fear as he knelt beside a man lying on the road.

‘I can't walk. I think my leg is broken,’ the injured man replied, his voice barely above a whisper.

Avinash reached out to help, but the man pushed him away with a weak gesture.

‘Leave me. You should go find a safe place. I'll manage on my own,’ he whimpered.

Reluctantly, Avinash rose to his feet and continued on his journey.

On his way, he saw the sight of all vehicles being made immobile by the vines. He heard someone trying to shout. But the voice was suppressed. He followed the voice and reached a wall covered with vines. In the darkness, he could just make out the muffled cries of someone in distress. With a mounting sense of horror, Avinash realized the truth. Trapped within the vines' grasp was a poor soul, bound and gagged. It would be only a matter of moments before the person suffocated to death. Without hesitation, Avinash turned and fled, the hushed echo of the victim's cries following him.

Avinash’s eyes were drawn to the haunting sight of the

buildings that had been consumed by the relentless advance of the vines. It was a scene straight out of a nightmare. It reminded Avinash of the archaeological sites he used to work on. The ancient structures he had excavated in the past had been weathered and worn, their crumbling frontages a testament to the passage of time. But here, in this city overtaken by darkness, the process of decay had been accelerated to a terrifying degree. Where once stood complex edifices, now lay twisted and deformed shapes, their walls obscured by a writhing mass of vines that seemed to pulse with a life of their own. The once-vibrant colours of the buildings had been swallowed by the encroaching darkness, leaving behind only a sickly hue that seemed to seep into the very air. The glass panels were shattered and destroyed. The hoardings and boards warped.

In the blink of an eye, centuries of history had been erased, replaced by a landscape of twisted vines and crumbling concrete. It was a sight that filled Avinash with a sense of profound unease, as if he were witnessing the end of days unfolding before his very eyes.

In the cover of darkness, Avinash saw a distant light. Like a primal man trying to reach for fire, Avinash ran to the source of the light. As he drew closer, however, the scene that unfolded before him was far from the sanctuary of warmth and safety he had imagined. Instead, he was met with a vision of destruction and chaos.

The light was actually a fierce blaze. It was a huge fire from a destroyed fuel pump. From the distance he saw the pump burning like a volcano. Avinash surveyed the scene before him. He saw a twisted wreckage of the fuel pump, its metal frame warped and charred by the intensity of the blaze. He could comprehend the fact that the vines must have destroyed the underground fuel tanks and some unknown subsequent sparks might have ignited the fuel.

But even as he watched, the flames began to falter and fade. Avinash could hardly believe his eyes as he witnessed the fire's sudden demise. He tried to comprehend the reason behind it. The vines, he understood, were not merely a force of destruction—they were guardians of the earth itself, protectors of its fragile balance and delicate equilibrium.

It was a revelation born from a fusion of scientific inquiry and primal intuition, a theory that sought to explain the inexplicable and make sense of the chaos that had unfolded before his eyes. In his mind's eye, Avinash envisioned a network of intricate passageways snaking their way through the earth like veins of an ancient monster, a labyrinthine maze of roots and vines that stretched deep into the bowels of the earth. These subterranean tendrils, he realized, had not only breached the underground fuel tanks but had also carved out a pathway for the volatile liquid to flow unchecked beneath the surface. But it was not merely the physical prowess of the vines that intrigued Avinash; it was their cunning and adaptability, their ability to manipulate the very fabric of the earth to suit their needs. With a deft touch, the vines had orchestrated a masterpiece of manipulation, coaxing the surrounding soil to compact and seal the breach, effectively smothering the flames before they could consume the precious fuel. Avinash understood one thing, that the vines would prevent pollution of any kind, even if it's toxic smoke from burning fuel.

Avinash pressed forward through the night-shrouded labyrinth of twisted vines and gnarled roots. The path ahead was fraught with peril, a treacherous gauntlet of obstacles that threatened to ensnare him in their clutches and drag him down into the abyss. The vines snaked and writhed like serpents in the gloom. Avinash could feel their ominous gaze upon him.

But it was not just the vines that posed a threat; it was the deep craters that dotted the landscape like festering wounds. Large sinkholes yawned hungrily beneath his feet, gaping maws that threatened to swallow him whole. In the inky darkness, Avinash could only imagine the horrors that lay concealed within their depths, hidden from sight but not from the imagination.

Avinash heard a tremor nearby. As his eyes scanned the desolate urbanscape, they were drawn to an apartment tower. The moon's wan light cast an ethereal glow upon the structure. Avinash gazed upon the towering monolith. He could see that the building seemed as though a tomb of twisted vines and creeping tendrils that coiled around its frame like serpents in the dark. Vines snaked their way up its walls, their tendrils burrowing into the concrete and glass.

And then he heard it - a tremor of impending doom. It started as a subtle vibration beneath his feet, a faint rumbling that reverberated through the earth like the heartbeat of some ancient Rakshasa stirring from its slumber.

Avinash's gaze snapped back to the building, his heart pounding like a drumbeat of dread. He watched in horror as cracks spiderwebbed across its surface like fissures. And then, with a deafening roar that shook the very foundations of the earth, the building began to crumble.

The sound was a discord of crashing concrete and shattering glass that drowned out the anguished cries of the doomed inhabitants within. Avinash staggered back, his ears ringing with the ear-splitting thunder of the collapsing structure. He watched in helpless horror as the building collapsed in on itself. It felt like a vortex of destruction that consumed everything in its path. Dust and debris filled the air, obscuring his vision in a choking haze of ash and smoke.

With a desperate cry, Avinash stumbled to safety. His instincts prevented him from getting injured by the debris.

Avinash trudged wearily through the darkened streets. His senses dulled by exhaustion, he felt the weight of the long day pressing down upon him. Though he had no way of knowing the hour, he could sense that it was late, perhaps around 3 AM, he estimated, but time seemed to have lost all meaning in the suffocating grip of the night. With each step, his limbs grew heavier, his movements sluggish and laboured. The events of the day, the horrors he had witnessed, the terror that had gripped the city, weighed upon him like a crushing burden.

Avinash stumbled forward with his eyes scanning the dimly lit streets for any sign of respite. He knew that he could go no further. His body cried out for rest.

Finding a patch of ground that seemed relatively free from the encroaching vines, Avinash collapsed onto his back, his limbs splayed out in exhaustion. He stared up at the sky, the canopy of stars shimmering overhead. In the absence of the city's harsh artificial lights, the night sky stretched out before him in all its breathtaking glory. Each twinkling star seemed to pulse with an otherworldly energy. For a fleeting moment, Avinash felt a sense of awe wash over him. But even as he marvelled at the beauty of the celestial display, he wondered, this is what the lights of the cityscape have hidden from us for all these years.

Something else that he had noticed is that the overwhelming presence of animals in the city. Where once there had been only the occasional stray cat or dog, now there were hordes of animals - cats and dogs, yes, but also hens, cows, goats, and pigs, their numbers swelling with each passing moment. Avinash watched the animals moving with an eerie sense of purpose, their eyes gleaming with a primal intelligence that belied their humble origins. They seemed to have escaped from the pens of slaughterhouses and farms.

Unfamiliar noises filled the air. Strange birds with iridescent plumage flitted through the trees, their haunting calls echoing through the night. Other creatures, unseen and unknown, emitted strange cries and calls.

Avinash succumbed to exhaustion. His mind plunged into a realm of twisted nightmares. In his dreams, he found himself navigating through the ancient ruins of a city long forgotten, its crumbling structures ensnared by suffocating vines. Avinash stumbled through the labyrinthine passages, his footsteps muffled by the dense undergrowth that carpeted the ground. Shadows danced and writhed in the flickering torchlight. As he ran forward, Avinash felt the weight of centuries bearing down upon him, the echoes of forgotten voices whispering in his ears. Each step he took seemed to bring him closer to the heart of the darkness that lay at the heart of the city, its secrets waiting to be unearthed by those foolhardy enough to seek them out.

But just as Avinash felt himself on the brink of discovery, he was suddenly jolted awake by a blinding light that flooded his vision. For a moment, he lay there in confusion. Slowly, he opened his eyes, blinking against the harsh glare of the daylight that streamed through the tangled foliage overhead. As his surroundings came into focus, Avinash realized with a jolt that he was no longer lost in the twisted depths of his nightmares, but standing on the precipice of a new day, a day fraught with its own terrors and uncertainties.

# 16

The cargo ship Tropical Voyager sailed through the inky darkness of the ocean, its massive hull slicing through the waves with ease. On board, Captain Stephen Mallory and his crew were on edge as they approached the port, which lay in the capital city of Kerala where they were scheduled to dock. But as they tried to establish communication with the port authorities, they were met with nothing but static.

'What the hell?' First Mate Mohit exclaimed, frustration evident in his voice as he adjusted the dials on the radio, trying desperately to make contact.

But no matter how many times they tried, there was no response from the other end. The airwaves remained eerily silent, devoid of any signs of life from the port authorities. Captain Mallory furrowed his brow, his mind racing with possibilities.

'This isn't right,' he muttered to himself, his voice barely audible over the sound of the wind and waves. 'Something's happened.'

The crew exchanged worried glances, a sense of unease settling over them like a thick fog. Without communication from the port, they were flying blind, unsure of what lay ahead.

'We can't just wait here,' Captain Mallory said, his voice firm. 'We need to make a decision.'

The crew nodded in agreement, their faces drawn with worry as they considered their options. With no word from the port authorities, they had no choice but to proceed cautiously. As the Tropical Voyager drew closer to the port, the crew peered anxiously into the darkness, searching for any signs of life. But all they saw was silence, broken only by the gentle lapping of the waves against the ship's hull. And then, as they finally reached the port and prepared to dock, they were met with a sight that made them freeze with wonder.

The port was eerily quiet, devoid of any signs of life. The buildings stood empty and abandoned. Their windows dark and empty. Cranes loomed overhead like skeletal sentinels, their metal frames rusted and worn. As the crew looked out across the water, they saw other ships and boats, their hulls covered with thick layers of vines and foliage.

'What the hell happened here?' Mohit whispered.

Captain Mallory shook his head, his mind reeling with disbelief.

With no other options left, the crew prepared to dock the

Horizon Voyager, their hearts heavy with dread. As they stepped onto the abandoned docks, they couldn't shake the feeling that they were walking into a nightmare.

The rising sun made the scene much more visible. The port was like a ghost town, its streets empty and silent. The buildings loomed overhead like silent watchtowers, their windows dark and foreboding. And everywhere they looked, they saw evidence of decay and neglect, as if the port had been abandoned for years.

'What happened here?' one of the crew members asked, his voice trembling with fear.

'Captain, do you think we should disembark here?' Mohit asked Captain Mallory.

'Listen up, men,' Captain Mallory said loudly, 'it doesn't feel right about this port. I'm getting some serious red flags here. It looks like there's been some kind of major incident or disaster. I don't want to take any chances with the safety of this vessel or our crew. Let's get out of here and find another port to dock. We'll radio ahead and see if we can get some info on what's going on, but for now, let's not stick around to find out. Prep the engines for departure and let's get moving.'

As the cargo ship Tropical Voyager attempted to leave the port, the crew soon realized that their vessel was not as seaworthy as they had hoped. The captain's voice crackled over the intercom, his tone laced with urgency and dread.

'We've got a serious problem here. The ship's propellers are entangled in some kind of thick, twisting vines. It looks like they've torn through the hull. We're taking on water fast. Brace yourselves!'

Panic gripped the crew like a vice as they scrambled to assess the damage and formulate a plan of action. But their efforts were in vain. The ship lurched violently, listing to one side as the relentless onslaught of vines continued to tear through its metal hull.

Screams pierced the air as the crew fought desperately to free the ship from the suffocating embrace of the encroaching plant life. With each passing moment, the ship sank lower into the depths, dragged down by the relentless grip of the vines from under the sea. Panic gave way to terror as the crew found themselves trapped in the suffocating darkness of the ocean, their lungs burning for air as the water closed in around them. Frantic cries for help echoed across the deck as crew members struggled to break free from the tangled mass of vegetation that now enveloped the bottom of the ship.

As the Tropical Voyager slipped beneath the waves, the crew found themselves dragged down into the abyss by the merciless grip of the vines. In the inky blackness of the ocean depths, their screams were swallowed by the void, their bodies crushed beneath the weight of the suffocating darkness.

*************

Darkness blanketed the world outside the Lord Mallikeshwar Temple, a sinister shroud that obscured the horrors lurking beyond its hallowed walls. Unlike most government-run temples in Kerala, this sacred place welcomed visitors of all faiths, drawing them in with promises of solace and sanctuary. For Professor Ahmed, it was a refuge in troubled times, a bastion of peace. But on this fateful night, he found himself alone in the temple's shadowy embrace, accompanied only by a handful of devoted priests who tended to its ancient sanctum. The calamity of the vines had spread like a plague across the state, driving most people into hiding behind the safety of locked doors and barricaded windows. Yet, Professor Ahmed, ever the seeker of truth, had ventured out into the darkness, drawn by an inexplicable force that whispered of danger and dread.

Parking his car at a safe distance, Professor Ahmed made his way to the temple on foot. Reaching the temple's entrance, Professor Ahmed paused to remove his footwear, a ritual gesture of respect and reverence. He had already left his electronic devices and leather belongings in the car, which was also a custom of the temple. Stepping over the threshold, he was enveloped in a world devoid of modern amenities, lit only by the flickering glow of torches and lanterns that cast shadows upon the ancient stone walls.

Outside, the carnage unfolded in silent horror, the vines twisting like serpents as they devoured everything in their path. Electric lamps lay shattered and abandoned, their feeble light extinguished by the insatiable hunger of the encroaching plant life. However, the temple remained untouched. Professor Ahmed's mind raced as he surveyed the scene before him, piecing together the fragments of information he had gathered in his quest for understanding. He knew all too well what was happening, for he had seen the signs of nature's wrath before. Turning his gaze inward,

Professor Ahmed sought solace in the familiar rituals of prayer and meditation, drawing strength from the ancient wisdom that resonated within the temple's hallowed halls.

****************

As the sun cast its feeble light upon the ravaged city, the military forces stirred from their camp in the city. In a desperate bid to reclaim the once-thriving metropolis from the clutches of the encroaching vines, they had been mobilized with nothing but raw steel and steely determination. However, they were devoid of any automobiles or equipment. Now, armed only with knives, choppers, and machetes, the soldiers rode into battle atop horses.

But as they entered the city, they realized the true extent of the challenge before them. They moved with purpose yet lacked direction, their orders vague and their objectives unclear. Back in the barracks, their comrades were already trying to clear the area of the vine attack. Despite their best efforts, the vines continued to advance. But following the orders above, these personnel just roamed the city without knowing what exactly to do. They knew very well that with their mere knives and machetes, they couldn’t clear the city of these vines.

The military forces, armed with nothing but their wits and the primitive weapons they could muster, ventured cautiously into the overgrown streets, their senses alert for any sign of danger. Among the twisting vines and tangled undergrowth, an unseen menace lurked, waiting patiently for its unsuspecting prey. Unbeknownst to the soldiers, they were walking into a trap laid by nature itself. As the soldiers moved deeper into the heart of the city, they began to notice strange movements in the foliage around them. Vines snaked out from the shadows. But it was not just the vines that posed a threat; hidden among them were the carnivorous plants, their deceptively innocent appearance belying their deadly nature.

Major Krishnakumar and his companions, Ajay and Tony, stumbled upon an alley veiled in thick foliage. As they ventured deeper into the alley, the men were ensnared by a haunting melody, a sweet, seductive tune that seemed to emanate from the very heart of the foliage. Mesmerized by the enchanting sound, they followed its siren call, their senses ensnared by the alluring scent that permeated the air. The scent was intoxicating, its sweetness irresistible, as if it held the promise of untold ecstasy. Each breath filled their lungs with the heady aroma, flooding their minds with euphoria and drowning out the nagging voice of reason.

Lost in a trance-like state, the men moved as though guided by some unseen force, their movements fluid and unhurried. The vines that surrounded them seemed to pulse with a life of their own, their tendrils weaving a hypnotic dance around the unsuspecting intruders. And then, emerging from the dense foliage before them, they beheld a sight that defied belief - a cavern adorned with delicate petals, its vibrant red interiors bathed in an ethereal glow. It was a scene of otherworldly beauty, beckoning them closer with its promise of hidden wonders. Driven by an insatiable curiosity, Major Krishnakumar and his companions stepped eagerly into the cavern, their hearts pounding with anticipation. But as they ventured deeper into its depths, a sense of unease began to gnaw at the edges of their consciousness. The cavern seemed to pulse with a malicious energy, its walls closing in around them with a suffocating intensity. Panic clawed at their throats as they realized the true nature of their surroundings - a trap cunningly disguised as a sanctuary of bliss. With a deafening snap, the cavern's jaws closed shut, revealing its true identity as a monstrous Venus Flytrap, its gaping maw poised to consume its unwitting prey. The men recoiled in horror, their screams echoing through the cavernous chamber as they struggled in vain against the plant's unyielding grasp. But it was futile. The Venus Flytrap held them fast, its voracious appetite sated by the taste of human flesh. A carnivorous plant of unparalleled horror, the Venus Flytrap in nature preyed upon insects and small creatures, but here they had mutated into monstrous proportions, thriving on a diet of human victims.

The Venus Flytraps weren't the only large carnivorous plants hunting humans in the city. The giant Pitcher Plants were equally insidious, their gaping maws hidden among the foliage, their sweet scent irresistible to the unsuspecting. As the soldiers drew near, they found themselves drawn inexorably towards the yawning chasms of the plants, unable to resist the lure of their deadly perfume. And then there were the Sundews, their sticky tendrils glistening in the dim light, ready to ensnare any unfortunate humans that strayed too close. With their deceptively delicate appearance, they seemed almost harmless, but beneath their innocent disguise lay a voracious appetite that could not be satisfied.

As the soldiers moved deeper into the heart of the city, they soon found themselves surrounded on all sides by the carnivorous plants, their movements hampered by the dense undergrowth and treacherous terrain. With each step they took, they risked falling victim to the deadly traps that lay hidden beneath the foliage, their cries of terror echoing through the deserted streets. But it was not just the plants that posed a threat; the very vines themselves seemed to come alive, twisting and writhing like serpents as they sought out their prey. With each passing moment, the soldiers found themselves ensnared in a deadly game of cat and mouse, their every move countered by the relentless advance of nature's fury. In the end, there was little they could do but fight for their lives. They struggled desperately to free themselves from the grasp of the carnivorous plants. But it was a futile effort.

*************

Meanwhile, the horror that had gripped Alma Fatima's neighbourhood seemed to have reached its peak with the break of dawn. As the first rays of sunlight struggled to penetrate the thick canopy of despair that hung over the area, Alma and her family found themselves trapped in a waking nightmare. Throughout the long and torturous night, the air had been filled with the anguished cries of their neighbours. But there was another audible phenomenon that happened lately. Noises of buildings collapsing.

'How in the hell are those houses getting destroyed?' asked Ajmal.

'These vines and creepers must have been destroying the

foundations of the buildings. That's the only way,' replied Nazeer.

Then they began to hear crumbling noises in their house as well. The house seemed to vibrate.

'What was that?' asked Alma with tearful eyes.

'Everyone, stay quiet,' hushed Afsal.

The sound of the concrete breaking apart and wood pieces tearing apart, accompanied by the cracks of the windows, could also be heard.

'I think we should get out of here?' said Nazeer.

'But it's not safe outside,' said Ajmal.

'The house will collapse any moment. Come, let's go!' Nazeer said sternly as he walked to the door. Alma and her mother followed.

As they walked, the house began to shake.

'Come on! Run!' yelled Nazeer.

With each step, the ground seemed to shift beneath their feet, threatening to swallow them whole as the earth trembled with the force of the encroaching horror. And then, in an instant, it happened. With a blaring clamour, their house collapsed around them, a twisted mass of concrete and steel crashing down with unstoppable force. Alma was thrown to the ground as she managed to jump outside the main door of the house.

All happened in a split second. She woke up beneath the debris of the house. She was outside. Hardly any hard materials crushed her. But that wasn't the case for her family. She saw her father dead after being impaled by an iron rod from a broken concrete shade. As for her mother and brothers, they were nowhere to be seen. Alma Fatima stood amidst the wreckage of what had once been her family's home. The sight before her was a cruel testament to the devastating power of the vines. Alma sank to her knees amidst the rubble. Her hands trembled as she reached out to touch the broken fragments of her former life. She cried for her mother and her brothers. Deep inside, she knew they were also dead like her father.

# 17

According to his followers, Karmadom Sahadevan, the Chief Minister of Kerala State, is a very courageous and ferocious man. He isn't afraid of gods or demons. He always claims to have walked beneath unsheathed swords and swum through canals of blood. There is also a true fact that he was the prime suspect in a political murder case fifty years ago.

However, there is a secret fear that lurks in the depths of the Chief Minister's heart, hidden beneath layers of stoic resolve. It is not the ghosts of past foes or the threat of future adversaries that make him shiver, but rather the humble palm civet, a creature no larger than a housecat.

Civets, with their elongated bodies and piercing eyes, are a common sight in the landscapes of Kerala. Yet, it is their mischievous nature that unnerves the Chief Minister. These creatures, with their penchant for mischief, have a peculiar habit of marking their territory with an unassuming stream of urine, a habit that has earned them the ire of the illustrious leader.

Indeed, Hill House, once a bastion of colonial grandeur dating back to the 19th century, bore witness to the whims of these nocturnal intruders. Their visits, marked by signs of soiled shirts and lingering odours, became a source of vexation for the Chief Minister, disrupting the sanctity of his abode and stirring a fear that belied his reputation.

Determined to reclaim his sanctuary from the clutches of these diminutive adversary, the Chief Minister took decisive action. With a stroke of his pen, he allotted a staggering sum of 50 million rupees from the government coffers to fortify the defences of the Chief Minister's Official Residence. He also installed an elevator in the two-story building.

Hill House underwent a transformation, its hallowed halls reborn as a fortress against the incursions of palm civets. High walls rose to deter would-be intruders, while intricate traps and deterrents were deployed with military precision. No expense was spared in the quest to safeguard the sanctity of the Chief Minister's domain.

Inside the modernized Hill House, the CM remained a prisoner within the walls of his own fortress. Since the devastating attack of the vines, he had not dared to venture beyond the safety of his residence. Alongside him were his wife, their loyal security guards, and a handful of trusted comrades. Communication with the outside world had been severed, leaving the CM cut off from his allies and the rest of the world.

As the Chief Minister's stress mounted, fuelled by the

uncertainty of their situation and the dwindling supplies within Hill House, provisions were running dangerously low.

The once-bustling halls of Hill House now lay silent and empty. The Chief Minister's wife moved about the residence like a ghost, her eyes haunted by the horrors that lurked just beyond their walls. The security guards maintained a vigilant watch, their nerves stretched taut as they awaited the next onslaught of the vines. The CM found himself grappling with doubts and fears that he had never before known. He questioned his decisions, wondering if there was more he could have done to prevent the catastrophe that had befallen their state.

The sounds of the armed security guards being dragged away by the vines around Hill House reached the CM. He surveyed the area from the balcony and saw the horrific sight of the security guards being tormented and dragged away by vines. The CM's heart pounded like a drum as he stood on the balcony, watching the chaos unfolding below. From the darkness below came the chilling sounds of his armed security guards, their shouts of terror drowned out by the merciless advance of the vines.

'CM, CM!' a frantic voice broke through the cacophony, as Jayarajan, one of his loyal comrades, rushed to his side.

The CM turned to face him, his eyes wide with alarm.

'Yes, I've seen it,' he replied grimly, his voice barely above a whisper.

'The vines... they're attacking everyone outside. It won't be long before they breach the walls of the house.' Jayarajan's breath came in ragged gasps as he spoke, his words tumbling out in a frantic rush.

'What should we do now?' the CM asked with desperation.

'We need to get to the panic room, the bunker,' Jayarajan urged, his eyes darting nervously towards the darkened corridors of the house. 'It's the only place we'll be safe.'

'And what about supplies? Food, water...' the CM nodded grimly.

'There are enough supplies inside the bunker to feed all of us for a week,' reassured Jayarajan.

'Okay, lead me to the bunker,' said the CM.

On their way, the CM's wife also joined them on the way to the bunker. Some other loyal comrades and his gunmen also followed him. As they reached the bunker, the CM entered the password in the panel in front of the steel door and it opened. The CM shouldered his way inside. When the others followed him, he stopped them by yelling 'Kadakk Purath!'

'Comrade, why?' asked Jayarajan.

'There may not be enough supplies. Who knows if this calamity would just last for a week?' replied the CM, and then he forcefully closed the bunker's door and locked it from inside.

The interior of the bunker had a comfortable bed. A closet stocked with food and water supplies lined one wall, while the walls were coated with tiles. The room was lit by battery-powered electrical lights. Apart from potential boredom, one could stay alone there for a few days without getting cabin fever.

As the Chief Minister sat lost in thoughts of his former glory, a sense of unease settled over him like a shroud. Ignoring the chaos outside, he allowed himself to drift into a false sense of security. Suddenly, the tranquillity of the bunker was shattered by an irritating sound – the unmistakable cry of a civet. His heart hammered as he scanned the room. Then, without warning, came the deafening crash of tiles falling to the ground. With mounting horror, the Chief Minister watched as sections of the walls around him crumbled away, revealing the concrete structure beneath.

Roots began to pierce through the fractured concrete, their gnarled tendrils reaching out. A sickening sense of dread washed over him as a burrow emerged from the depths, followed by the eerie sight of civets slipping through the opening. Despite his best efforts to stifle the rising panic within him, the Chief Minister couldn't suppress a scream as the civets swarmed into the room. To his surprise, however, they showed no signs of aggression towards him. Instead, they encircled him.

But before he could make sense of this bizarre turn of events, more burrows began to appear, sprouting up like sinister weeds around him. He realized that he was completely surrounded, the civets closing in from all sides. Then, as if on cue, the vines began to slither into the room through the newly formed burrows. The Chief Minister watched as the roots cracked through the concrete walls, snaking their way towards him like serpents of doom. Paralyzed with fear, he could only watch helplessly as the vines closed in around him, their suffocating embrace threatening to crush the life from his body.

More roots cracked the concrete walls and snaked inside. From each corner vines came and each one coiled around the limbs of the CM and it started pulling him to each corner. The CM cried in pain. The pulling force increased. The civets encircled the CM watching what's unfolding in front of them. Just like how a medieval torture was done, the vines pulled the CM's limbs, dismembering him and killing him painfully.

*************

In the eerie twilight of the backwaters, Ragesh Nakutty stood paralyzed with fear on the balcony of his luxurious lakeside home while the setting sun cast long shadows across the landscape. The living vines, twisted and malevolent, encroached upon his house, the tendrils snaking their way through the cracks in the walls and creeping ever closer to where he stood. He had heard about the stories of what the vines are capable to do through his comrades.

With each passing moment, the vines drew nearer, their unyielding advance driving him to the brink of madness. His comrades, those who had not already met a grisly fate at the hands of the encroaching vegetation, had abandoned him to his fate, leaving him to face the horror alone. Desperation gnawed at his insides as he frantically searched for a means of escape. His gaze fell upon the vast expanse of the lake before him. Without hesitation, Ragesh made a split-second decision. He would flee to the water, seeking refuge from the vines that sought to claim him.

With a surge of adrenaline, Ragesh bolted from his home. Behind him, the vines slithered and twisted, their hungering tendrils reaching out to ensnare him. He reached the edge of the lake just as the first of the vines closed in around him, their grasping fingers mere inches from him. With a desperate leap, Ragesh hurled himself into the small boat moored nearby, his heart raced as he fumbled for the oars.

As he rowed with all his might, the sound of the vines grew fainter and fainter. Ragesh collapsed onto the wooden planks of the boat in exhaustion. He lied there, trying to catch his breath. I need to stay here until things are finally over.

Ragesh Nakutty heard an irritating noise, something scratching on the boat. He got up and saw vines from the depths of the lake has attached to the boat. Within a few moments, the entire boat is covered by vines. Ragesh Nakutty knew everything is over. But in that desperate moment, it wasn't his childhood memories that flashed before him. Instead, he felt the pain of the innocent calf which he butchered with a blunt knife in public to make a political statement.

Ragesh watched as the vines slithered their way over the sides of the boat. Before he could react, the vines had ensnared him, their grip like iron as they coiled around his limbs and pulled him into their grasp. Ragesh felt the vines begin to encroach upon him slithering over his skin like a thousand tiny serpents. He tried to fight back, to break free from their suffocating embrace, but it was pointless. The vines began to invade his very body. They coiled around his arms and legs, squeezing tighter and tighter until he could barely breathe. And then, with a sudden, agonizing pressure, two of the vines forced their way into his ears, while two more wriggled their way up his nostrils, burrowing deep into his skull.

Ragesh screamed in pain and terror as the vines invaded his senses. He felt as if he were being torn apart from the inside out, his very essence consumed by the relentless onslaught of the plant's assault. As the vines tightened their grip, Ragesh's vision began to blur and fade, his consciousness slipping away into the abyss. Another strand of vine entered his mouth, went split apart and one strand when down through his oesophagus and the other one through his windpipe. The strand of vines that went through his oesophagus entered his stomach and slithered through his intestines and exited through his anus while the one that went to his windpipe began disrupting his lungs.

In his final moments, all he could hear was the echoing laughter of the vines, mocking him as they dragged him down into the depths of the lake, never to be seen again.

*************

In the heart of the lush, verdant valley of the Western Ghats stood the gigantic structure of the Thumpaperiyar Dam. For the people of Kerala, it was not just a structure of concrete and steel. For generations, it had stood as a guardian, holding back the rushing waters of the Thumpaperiyar River and providing vital irrigation and water resources to the surrounding farmlands and communities. The Dam is vital and crucial. People always held concerns about it as just a slight failure from this dam can mean destruction of four districts of Kerala by being flooded and submerged completely. But beneath it, a sinister force had been at work, silently gnawing away at its foundations and sowing the seeds of destruction. Deep within the earth, hidden from sight, the roots and vines had begun their insidious assault.

Despite the absence of electricity, the engineers and workers who tended to the dam remained steadfast in their duty. As the hours passed, a creeping sense of unease that seemed to seep into every crevice and corner of the structure. Then, without warning, the silence was shattered by the worrying sound of cracking and groaning metal.

The workers exchanged anxious glances as they realized the gravity of the situation. Metal gears and pipes twisted and contorted before their eyes, their once-sturdy frames no match for the relentless onslaught of the vines and roots.

Panic began to spread among the workers as they scrambled to assess the damage and formulate a plan of action. But it was already too late. The vines had struck with ruthless efficiency where they wreaked havoc on critical metal components with alarming speed. With each passing moment, the situation grew direr. The workers found themselves powerless to stop the relentless advance of the vines. Desperation took hold as the engineers and workers realized the futility of their efforts. The vines had made their tools and equipment useless.

The employees panicked. They didn't know what to do. Within moments, they heard loud cracks and they saw for themselves, the cracks being formed in the mega arch dam. They braced themselves. It's too late to do anything.

As the cracks in the dam widened with a thunderous roar, the towering structure of the Thumpaperiyar Dam buckled under the immense pressure, sending shockwaves reverberating across the verdant valley. With a resounding crash, the dam gave way, unleashing a mega tsunami that surged forth with unstoppable force. The rushing waters gushed downward like a colossal waterfall, sweeping aside everything in its path with terrifying ferocity. Entire villages were engulfed in an instant as the waves surged forward, obliterating everything in its wake.

In a matter of seconds, the landscape was transformed into a scene of unimaginable devastation. Houses were torn from their foundations, their shattered remains swept away in the relentless deluge. Malls, apartments, parks, all were consumed by the raging waters, reduced to nothing more than debris floating on the surface.

The destruction spread like wildfire, engulfing entire districts in its path. People who had sought refuge in their homes found themselves trapped and helpless as the floodwaters rose around them, swallowing them whole in a cruel and merciless embraces. The cries of the doomed echoed through the valley.

# 18

Far away from the cities, in the forests and rugged mountains, there exists a tradition as old as time itself, the practice of naked asceticism among Hindu Yogis. They lead a life of simplicity and spiritual dedication. Popularly known as Naga Sadhus, they live by forsaking worldly possessions and comforts to seek enlightenment in the lap of nature.

The origins of the Naga Sadhus can be traced back to ancient times. It is believed that the earliest Naga Sadhus imparted the sacred knowledge of yoga from Lord Shiva himself who is the Supreme Yogi and the embodiment of asceticism. The Naga Sadhus follow a similar path inspired by the teachings of Lord Shiva by renouncing material possessions and societal norms to delve deep into the realms of spiritual practice. According to their beliefs, one can better connect with the divine and attain a state of ultimate liberation by shedding all layers of clothing and material attachments.

The Naga Sadhus immerse themselves in rigorous practices

of meditation, yoga, and austerity while living in remote caves, dense forests, and secluded ashrams. For the Naga Sadhus, nudity symbolizes the shedding of all illusions and the embrace of ultimate truth. By stripping away the layers of clothing, they strive to strip away the layers of ego and desire that obscure the true nature of the self. In this state of nakedness, they seek to attain a state of pure consciousness and union with the divine.

Throughout history, the Naga Sadhus have played a pivotal role in the preservation and propagation of Hindu culture and spirituality. They have been known to rise up in times of crisis, defending the Dharma and protecting the sanctity of Hindu temples and traditions.

Overwhelmed by materialistic rudiments, some modern humans also seek refuge in nature by joining the cult of Naga Sadhus. Suresh Tiwari was one of them.

Meanwhile, there were a few people who were detached from earth, literally.

In the eerie silence of space, the astronauts aboard the International Space Station found themselves gripped by an unsettling sense of dread. For days, they had been met with nothing but static on their communication systems.

'What's going on down there?' Commander Root asked with his voice crackling over the intercom. 'Why aren't they responding?'

'I don't know, sir,' replied Lieutenant Sharma. 'We've tried every frequency, every channel. There's nothing.'

A sense of fear settled over the crew as they gathered in

the cramped confines of the control room as their faces illuminated by the soft glow of the monitors.

'We can't just sit here and wait,' declared Dr. Ramirez, the station's chief scientist. 'We need to figure out what's going on.'

'But how?' asked Lieutenant Sharma. 'We're stranded up here, millions of miles from home. We don't have the resources to investigate.'

Commander Root paced the room, his mind racing with thoughts of the worst-case scenario.

'We'll conduct a full diagnostic of the station, check every system, every component. There has to be a logical explanation for this,' said Commander Root.

The crew set to work as tensions ran high. Every creak and groan of the station's structure seemed to echo through the corridors like a bad omen. Hours turned into days as the astronauts worked tirelessly to uncover the source of the communication blackout. But despite their best efforts, the mystery remained unsolved, leaving them with a fretting sense of unease.

The crew exchanged uneasy glances. Their fear grew with each passing moment. Despite their best efforts, they received no communication from earth. With heavy hearts, the crew watched helplessly on the blank communication devices, leaving them adrift in a sea of uncertainty. As the realization sank in that they were truly alone, a sense of despair washed over them, their dreams of returning home shattered. In the cold, unforgiving expanse of space, the astronauts of the International Space Station were left to confront their worst fears. And as the darkness of space closed in around them, they braced themselves for the horrors that awaited them in the endless abyss.

*************

Back on earth, Alma survived the collapse of her house, walked away with minimal injuries. She stumbled along the shattered remnants of her neighbourhood. On her way, she was greeted with more collapsing houses and more dead bodies on the street. With each step, Alma's hope dwindled. As she reached the main road, she saw the once bustling road was now a desolate wasteland, choked with creeping vines and twisted metal. Abandoned cars lay scattered like discarded toys with their windows shattered and their frames crushed.

However, there are others who were on their way to refuge. A massive exodus. Alma searched for a familiar face but there were none. She sat on the side of the road, exhausted. She sank to the ground. Alma realized that she will witness her end of life among this crowd of people. She knew that her death will correspond to the end of mankind. She was lost in her thoughts unaware of what is happening around her.

Alma Fatima

Alma

'Alma!'

She heard a familiar voice and turned to its source.

'Avinash!' she gasped.

Avinash was in as bad shape like her. Sweaty, bruised and wounded.

'How did you find me?' she asked.

'Deus Ex Machina, maybe?' he laughed.

'This isn't a story, though,' she also laughed with a tear rolling from her eyes.

'I was just walking towards your house's location you once told me. Didn't expect to see you on the way,' he said, panting.

'What happened to you?' she asked.

'What happened to you too?' he mirrored.

Suddenly, they heard a collective noise of cries and screams. It was accompanied by the noise of thousands of vines and roots slithering through the earth. In the distance, the survivors watched in horror as the vines descended upon their fellow humans. The scene grew more chaotic and surreal. The survivors scrambled to their feet as they fled in terror. No matter how fast they ran, no matter how far they tried to escape, the vines were always one step ahead. They snaked through the streets like serpents, ensnaring their victims.

The survivors cried out in agony as the vines tightened their grip, their screams echoed. Limbs were torn apart, bodies crushed beneath the unyielding onslaught of nature's fury.

Alma and Avinash didn't run. They watched the horrific scene unfold.

Alma hugged Avinash.

'So, this is the end?' she asked.

For Avinash, time stood still.

The profound teachings of the Vedas, the ancient scriptures that had shaped his understanding of the universe since his childhood days in the Balasadanam whirl pooled in the quiet depths of his mind. The rise and fall of empires, the shifting sands of time that erode even the mightiest monuments. The wisdom of Hindu philosophy that resonated with Avinash's soul came back. The teachings of Maya, the illusory nature of reality that veils the true essence of existence. In the grand cosmic drama of life, Maya is the veil that separates the individual soul from its divine source, leading it on a journey of self-discovery and spiritual evolution. The concept of cosmic destruction by Lord Shiva in his form as the great destroyer. In the grand scheme of creation, destruction is not an end but a necessary precursor to new beginning.

For in the timeless wisdom of Hindu philosophy, Avinash remembered a profound truth that the journey of the soul is a sacred pilgrimage, guided by the eternal principles of Dharma, Karma, and Moksha. And though the path may be fraught with obstacles and challenges, the destination remains unchanged. It is the realization of our divine nature and the ultimate union with the cosmic consciousness that lies at the heart of all creation.

Avinash came back into consciousness, resuming his sight on the chaos in front of him. He saw dogs, cats and birds all peacefully roaming around without being attacked by the vines. Avinash just needed a few more seconds to connect everything together.

'What are you doing?' asked Alma, perplexed, as Avinash violently unhooked her hijab and threw it away. The black piece of cloth flew past yards as the ever beautiful face of Alma Fatima was revealed.

'Undress! Now!' Avinash replied as he frantically began unbuttoning his shirt.

'What!! What do you mean?' asked Alma, still in wonder.

'I have no time to explain. Please do as told. Let's see what happens!' said Avinash as he unzipped his jeans and removed it with considerable effort.

Meanwhile, Alma had tough time removing her clothing as it had multiple layers.

Being completely naked after removing his underwear, Avinash assisted Alma by unhooking her bra from behind. He noticed the vines approaching them in a greater speed.

'What now?' Alma blurted.

'Remove the ornaments,' Avinash yelled.

'But they are gold!'

He didn't bother to reply as he used his energy to remove her bangles and rings.

As Alma was removing the earing of her left ear, Avinash assisted in removing the one from the right ear.

The violent merciless vines were just fifty feet from them.

'Remove your nose ring!' Avinash said with fear in his voice.

'I can't! It's stuck!' Alma cried.

Avinash tried to remove it, but it was indeed stuck.

The vines were just twenty feet from them, fast approaching.

Alma twisted, pulled, pushed, swirled, spun and did whatever she could, but the nose ring was still stuck.

The vines were just ten feet from them, with sharp edges.

Avinash, with all his effort, took a grip on her nose ring and pulled it with all his might, removing it, tearing Alma's nose in the process accompanied with her loud cry of pain.

The vines slithered towards Alma and Avinash, and just rested there without attacking them. Avinash and Alma panted. The sweaty naked bodies hugged. They were alone, surrounded by the dead bodies of humans.

Alma and Avinash walked through the city. But it doesn't look like a city anymore. The large buildings were overwhelmed by vegetation. There were absolutely no artificial things in sight. It appeared to be a large jungle. They heard the sounds of wild animals from the zoo, walking freely in the city. In plain sight, they saw a tiger prowling in the distance.

The couple were searching for fellow survivors. It is possible that there may be others who also found the secret of survival. However, no human noise was heard.

Until they heard a cry.

It wasn't a cry of an adult but that of a baby.

Alma and Avinash rushed to the source of the cry and it was a destroyed hut in the edge of a slum. The dead bodies of humans can be seen being devoured by the foliage. Amongst them, they saw a naked infant crying in a bamboo cradle.

Alma took the baby and looked at Avinash. He smiled.

The couple walked, barefoot, on the lush foliage of the once asphalt road, in search of other humans who have found the way to join nature and survived.

The couple walked away to an undecided destination, each step, taken barefoot, connected them more deeply to the pulse of the earth beneath their feet. The air was thick with the scent of rich soil and fragrant blossoms. They walked in search of other humans who had found solace in the bosom of nature.

The familiar noise of the motor, drills, horns and traffics were absent. Instead, they were greeted by the warmth of the sun on their skin, the rustle of leaves in the breeze, the chorus of echoing birdsong.

# About the Author

**Yadu Vijayakrishnan** is a filmmaker, cinematographer, and writer. At the age of 19, he worked as one of the cinematographers on the Brazilian film "Feio, Eu?" and subsequently made several short films before completing his graduation. He directed and produced over twenty historical documentaries and a fifty-episode travelogue series for a TV channel over two years.

Yadu directed the documentary "21 Months of Hell," which portrayed the torture methods employed by the government during the Emergency period in India. Following this, he worked as the cinematographer for two films and directed two horror web series. He then directed the Sanskrit movie "Bhagavadajjukam," which had its world premiere at the International Film Festival of India and was screened at the Bangalore International Film Festival, BRICS Shanghai Film Festival, New York Indian Film Festival, Kolkata International Film Festival, and Rajasthan International Film Festival.

Yadu Vijayakrishnan serves as an Advisory Panel Member of the Central Board of Film Certification under the Ministry of Information and Broadcasting, Government of India. "The Story of Ayodhya" is his debut novel.

www.ingramcontent.com/pod-product-compliance
Lightning Source LLC
LaVergne TN
LVHW091318150826
845673LV00006B/1696